I0616725

IF I WERE KING

JUSTIN HUNTLY McCARTHY

1st WORLD
LIBRARY
Literary Society

If I Were King

Justin Huntly McCarthy

© 1st World Library – Literary Society, 2004
PO Box 2211
Fairfield, IA 52556
www.1stworldlibrary.org
First Edition

LCCN: 2004195332

Softcover ISBN: 1-4218-0163-9
Hardcover ISBN: 1-4218-0063-2
eBook ISBN: 1-4218-0263-5

Purchase *"If I Were King"*
as a traditional bound book at:
www.1stWorldLibrary.org/purchase.asp?ISBN=1-4218-0163-9

1st World Library Literary Society is a nonprofit organization dedicated to promoting literacy by:

- Creating a free internet library accessible from any computer worldwide.
- Hosting writing competitions and offering book publishing scholarships.

**Readers interested in supporting literacy through sponsorship, donations or membership please contact:
literacy@1stworldlibrary.org
Check us out at: www.1stworldlibrary.ORG
and start downloading free ebooks today.**

If I Were King
contributed by Tim, Ed & Rodney
in support of
1st World Library Literary Society

DEDICATION

To Her

Through Whom and For Whom

This Book was Written

"The Loveliest Lady this side of Heaven."

XXI. XII. MCMI.

If I were king - ah love, if I were king!
What tributary nations would I bring
To stoop before your sceptre and to swear
Allegiance to your lips and eyes and hair.
Beneath your feet what treasures I would fling: -
The stars should be your pearls upon a string,
The world a ruby for your finger ring,
And you should have the sun and moon to wear
If I were king.

Let these wild dreams and wilder words take
wing,
Deep in the woods I hear a shepherd sing
A simple ballad to a sylvan air,
Of love that ever finds your face more fair.
I could not give you any godlier thing
If I were king.

CHAPTER I

IN THE FIRCONE TAVERN

In the dark main room of the Fircone Tavern the warm June air seemed to have lost all its delicacy, like a degraded angel. It was sodden through and through, as with the lees of wine; it was stained and shamed with the smells of hams and cheeses; it was thick and heavy as if with the breaths of all the rogues and all the vagabonds that had haunted the hostelry from its evil dawn. Such guttering lights and glimmering flames as lit the place - for there was a small fire on the wide hearth in spite of the fine weather - peopled the gloom with fantastic quivering shadows as of lean fingers that unfolded themselves to filch, or clenched themselves to stab in the back. But its patrons seemed to like the place well enough in spite of its miasma, and Master Robin Turgis, the fat landlord, drowsy with his own wine and dripping from the heat, surveyed them complacently, and wallowed as it were in the rattle and clink of mug and can, the full-throated laughter and the shrill chatter, crisply emphasized by oaths, which assured him of the Fircone's popularity with its intimates. Master Robin's intelligence was limited; his wit was simple; the processes of his mind moved easily along the lines of least resistance. The Burgundians might be hammering with mailed fists at the walls of Paris; the fire-new crown of Louis the Eleventh might be falling from the royal forehead: it mattered not a jot to dishonest Robin so long as the Fircone brimmed with company.

There was enough company in the room on this evening to content even his wish. It was not the kind of company that a wise man would desire to keep, but it delighted the innkeeper, for it drank deeply and spent freely, and in Robin's view it was of no more concern to him how the money that changed hands was come by than it was how the profound potations might affect the brains and stomachs of his clients. If any officer of the law had questioned him as to his association with a certain mysterious Brotherhood of the Cockleshells whose plunderings and pilferings were the pride of the Court of Miracles and the fear of citizens with strong boxes, he would have shrugged his fat shoulders and shaken his round head and disowned all knowledge of any such unlawful corporation. Yet his face wrinkled with smiles as his glance rested amiably upon the bodily presences of certain illustrious members of the brotherhood, wild men in withered frippery, wine-stained to the very bones.

They were five in number, and four of them were huddled round a table in the cosiest corner of the room, the corner that was sheltered from the heat of the fire by the high-backed settle, the corner that was nearest to the main door if one desired - as one often did - to slip out in a hurry, and to the red-curtained windows, if one desired - as one seldom did - a mouthful of fresh air. Robin Turgis knew them all, admired them all, feared them all, and yet he held head against them because his Beaune wine was so adorable, and because he could keep his own counsel. Slender René de Montigny, in a jerkin of rubbed and faded purple velvet, with his malign, Italianate face and his delicate Italianate grace; rotund Guy Tabarie, bluff, red and bald; Casin Cholet, tall and bird-like, with the figure of a stork and the features of a bird of prey; Jehan le Loup, who looked as vulpine as his nickname; these Robin Turgis eyed and catalogued with a kind of pride. It was a fearsome privilege for the Fircone to boast such patronage. On the settle, with his face to the fire, Colin de Cayeulx sprawled in a drunken sleep, forgetting and forgotten, a harmless looking, good-natured looking knave who was neither harmless nor good-natured.

For every man of the gang there was a woman, and there was a woman over, who was easily the central star of the flaunting galaxy. The shabby bravery of the men was matched by the shabby bravery of five out of the six women. Gaudy, painted, assertive strumpets with young, fair, shameless faces - worthy Jills of the ill-favoured Jacks who cuddled them - Jehanneton, the fair helm-maker; Denise, Blanche, Isabeau, and Guillemette, the landlord's daughter, who consorted gaily enough with these brightly-plumaged birds of a rogue's paradise. But the sixth woman was a bird of quite another feather.

Over all the clatter this woman's voice rose suddenly as clear as the call of a thrush, and the hot space seemed to cool and the hot air to clean as she sang. She who sang was a girl of five and twenty, whom it had pleased to clothe her ripe womanhood in a boy's habit, that clasped her fine body as close as a second skin, and she might have passed for a man no otherwhere than in a madhouse. She looked very charming in the stained and faded daintiness of her male attire. She wore a green velvet doublet and green woollen hose, with a scarlet girdle and pouch about her waist, and a scarlet feather stuck defiantly in her green cap, beneath which her long fair hair tumbled in liberal confusion about her shoulders. She sat on the edge of a table swinging one shapely leg loose and strained upon its fellow while she nursed her lute as if it had been a baby, and carolled as if there were no other work in the world to do than to sing. The men and women who sat and sprawled around the table kept quiet, listening to her and staring at her; sleepy Colin pricked his ears; Robin Turgis was alert to hear, for he knew that it was worth while to listen when Huguette du Hamel chose to sing. Robin Turgis knew all about her. Her gentle blood was wild blood, and in spite of her birth and her name she had drifted on the stream of strange pleasure to be the idol of the Fircone's shrine. Her voice was sweet and the tune had a tender, appealing grace, with a little minor wail in it that brought tears into the singer's eyes, and she mouthed the words as if she found them sweet as honey. And this is what she sang:

> "Daughters of pleasure, one and all,
>   Of form and feature delicate,
> Of bodies slim, and bosoms small,
>   With feet and fingers white and straight,
> Your eyes are bright, your grace is great
>   To hold your lovers' hearts in thrall;
> Use your red lips before too late,
>   Love ere love flies beyond recall."

Her voice dropped and her fingers tinkled over the strings. René de Montigny turned his dark, well-featured face in a sweeping leer that seemed to taste the familiar graces with gusto. "Devilish good advice, Dollies," he shouted, and as he spoke he hugged the nearest girl close to him, and tilting up her chin with his free hand, kissed her noisily. The girl squealed a little at his roughness; the other pairs laughed and clasped after his example, only the singer, unheeding, lifted her sweet voice again, and this time there was a savour of gall in the sweetness of the honey:

"For soon the golden hair is grey,
  And all the body's lovely line
In wrinkled meanness slipped astray;
  The limbs so round and ripe and fine
Shrivelled and withered; quenched the shine
  That made your eyes as bright as day:
So, ladies, hear these words of mine,
  Love, ere love flutter far away."

The drift of the music seemed sadder than before, and there was a little silence when the last words floated away into the blackened rafters, a silence broken by one of the girls.

"Enne, that was a sad song, Abbess," Isabeau sighed, and her face seemed to have paled beneath its false colours and the lines about her mouth and eyes to have grown older in surrender to inevitable thoughts. She whom the girl called Abbess laughed, and her mirth sounded harshly after the dreamy sweetness of her song.

"Master François Villon made it for me t'other day," she answered. "' You will grow old, Idol,' he said, 'and I make you this song to teach you true things.'"

Guy Tabarie, whose red hair bunched out like little flames from the fiery sun of his countenance, clapped his hands to the girl's waist and thrust his face near to hers. "Kiss me and forget it," he hiccoughed. The girl gave importunacy a little push which sent him staggering back to his seat. "I have no kisses for any Jack of you all but François," she said, while the others roared at the man's discomfiture. "Ah, there is no one of you that can write songs like him, or make one sad as he can in the midst of gladness."

The girl whom purple-coated René had kissed so rudely shivered a little. "A strange reason for liking a man," she whispered, "that he make you sad." She glanced wistfully round at her companions: to the faces of the women the influence of the song had lent an unwonted softness, but had brought no touch of tenderness to those of the men. Jehan le Loup banged his fist heavily on the table in furious protestation till the cans and flagons rattled.

"Is this a Court of Love?" he grunted, baring his yellow tusks in a swinish rage. "There are other rooms for love-making," and he jerked his thumb towards the roof. "We are here for drinking; we are here for dicing; to the devil with smocks and sonnets."

He jumbled the ivories lustily as he growled and the familiar jingle banished unfamiliar fancies. He slapped the spotted cubes on the table and as they rolled into equilibrium eager eyes counted them, and fingers eager or reluctant pinched or pushed at coins. The spell of the music was broken. The melodious Abbess, with eyes now glittering and tearless, swung her supple body from table to bench, thrust herself a place among the players, shouted to Robin Turgis to bring more wine, and spreading some silver on the dingy board surrendered to speculation. Nobody heeded the faint clink which told that a hand troubled the latch of the street door; nobody heeded the faint creaking which showed that it was being softly opened; nobody heeded the man who put his head gently through the opening and looked thoughtfully around him. The new-comer was a grim-visaged fellow, somewhere near the edge of middle age. He was dressed in the sober habit of a simple burgess, and he used the long fold that hung from his cloth cap very dexterously to hide his face. He peered into the obscurity of the room with a disquieting smile that deepened in its unpleasing expression as its owner surveyed the noisy fellowship in the corner, and nodded his head as he seemed to identify its members. Confident that nobody marked him he stealthily entered the room, and holding the door ajar, he motioned to one who still stood without to enter. The summons was answered by the entrance of another figure, capped and habited like the first, who slipped in swiftly and furtively, and made at once for the farthest and loneliest angle of the room without looking to right or left, while his herald, after closing the door as noiselessly as possible, followed quickly in his footsteps. If Master Robin, dancing attendance upon his clamourous customers, could have divined the identity of the newcomers whose advent he regarded so indifferently, his purple face would have paled and his stomach failed him at the thought that the Fircone sheltered the baleful presence of the king and of his malign satellite, Tristan l'Hermite.

The two strangers seated themselves at a small table in the very pole of the room to the place where the Abbess and her friends were busy, and the second of the pair, drawing a little apart the dark-coloured fold of cloth that almost concealed his features, looked around him curiously.

"Is this the eyrie?" he whispered, and his companion

answered him in the same low tone, "This is the Fircone Tavern, sire." The other's finger was lifted to his lip at once in warning. "Hush, gossip, hush," he muttered. "No title now, I beg of you. Here I am not Louis of France, but a simple sober citizen like yourself. I suppose we must take something for the good of the house?" His henchman promptly replied that such action was indispensable. But Louis still looked doubtful. "Will the liquor be very detestable," he asked, inserting two thin fingers in the black pouch at his belt. Tristan shook his head. "Nay, you can get good wine here if you know how to ask for it - and how to pay for it."

"No one knows better than I how to ask for anything," chuckled the king. "Or worse, how to for it," Tristan sneered. The king scowled at him. "Then, why do you keep my service?" he snapped. Tristan shrugged his shoulders. "Some dregs of devotion, I suppose. Here stands Master Innkeeper." For by this time Robin Turgis was at their elbow, scanning them narrowly with his small, pig - like eyes that could make little, however, of the well-muffled faces. He waited on their order with a kind of ferocious submission, draining his rank forehead with a sweep of his dirty palm.

"Friend," said Louis, sniffing sardonically at the too odoriferous personality of the taverner, "you behold here two decent cits who have turned a penny, or twain in a bargain, and have a mind to wet their whistles in consequence. Have you aught to offer that is good alike for purse and palate?"

Robin Turgis nodded his round head and fondled his round stomach. "We have a white wine of Beaune," he said unctuously, as if he were tasting the wares he commended, "at two sols the flagon that is noble drinking."

The king's sense of economy shivered at the sum; as if it had been a wound.

"Pasques-Dieu!" he stammered. "So it should be at the price." Robin Turgis remained unmoved: Tristan clinched the business. "Bring it," he said decisively, and as the landlord shambled away towards his cellar, Tristan met the king's condemnatory frown squarely.

"I wear out my hands and feet in your service," lie said, "I want to save my throat and stomach."

Louis made no answer and was mournfully silent until the obese landlord returned with the much-vaunted vintage, which he set down on the table with a brace of goblets. Louis fumbled with reluctant fingers in his pouch, extracted the exact amount necessary for payment and dropped it into the fat paw of Robin Turgis. But Robin lingered and Louis looking at him in surprise met the admonishing glare of Tristan. "Give him a penny for himself," Tristan whispered, and the king, with an unwillingness he was at no pains to conceal, added the demanded drink-money to the other coins, and eyed the departing back of the landlord with well-defined aversion. "You are generous with other people's pennies, friend," he snapped at his companion, but Tristan, paying no heed to his querulousness, filled the two cups with the clear golden liquid and thrust one of them under the nose of the sulky monarch. Its fine dry fragrance soothed Louis; he took a deep sip and was mollified; another and he had forgiven if not forgotten his generosity. He winked at Tristan amiably over the rim of the goblet. "This is seeing life, friend

Tristan," he murmured, contentedly, stretching his thin legs in delicious ease. But Tristan was in no holiday humour.

"Let's hope it mayn't be seeing death, friend Louis" he snorted. "There are a couple of rogues in that covey who would spit you or split you or slit you for the price of a drink."

Louis laughed affably. "And no such cheap bargain," he commented, "seeing what wine costs here. But this is an interesting business."

Tristan would concede nothing to the king's good-humour. "Where's the interest?" he asked. "A few bullies, bawds and bonarobas boozing together. You can keep the same company at court - only a shade cleaner - and not be out of pocket for the privilege either."

The king's mouth puckered in appreciation of some memory. He leaned forward and touched Tristan's sleeve.

"Gossip Tristan, there is at my court a scholar who told me an Eastern tale."

"Pray God it be a gay one such as your majesty loves,"

"Hush, man; no 'Majesty' here. 'Tis of an Eastern King, one Haroun, surnamed, as I shall be surnamed, The Just."

Tristan grunted sceptically, but Louis, ignoring the ejaculation, went on.

"It was his pastime to go about Bagdad of nights in disguise, and mingling with his people learn much to the advantage of the realm. I am following his example, and I expect to learn much in my turn."

Tristan looked pityingly at the complacent king. "You are likely to learn how unpopular you are, which I could have told you without this trouble; and you will be lucky if you do not get your throat cut into the bargain."

Something almost like a smile disturbed the familiar composure of the king's wrinkles. He took another sip of the wine and his affability expanded. "You are always a bird of evil omen," he chirped. "Be bright, man; look at me. The Burgundian Leaguer is at my gates; my throne sways like a rocking-chair, yet I don't pull a sad face."

"It's a good thing that somebody is pleased," Tristan commented. "Yes," said Louis, opening out his thin hands and studying their palms attentively, "I am pleased - " Tristan interrupted him roughly. "Pleased that the Burgundians threaten you outside the walls of Paris; pleased that Thibaut d'Aussigny bullies you inside the walls of Paris; pleased that your soldiers are mutinous; pleased that your citizens are sullen; by my faith, here are four royal reasons for a royal pleasure."

Louis shook his head playfully at his servant's grumbling. "Gossip Tristan," he asked, "do you know why I have come to this hovel to-night? I do not walk abroad like a king-errant in mere idleness of mind. I have come to learn what company my lord the Grand Constable keeps." Tristan's shaggy eyebrows arched in surprise as the king continued: "Our good Olivier assures us that our dear Thibaut d'Aussigny has taken it into his head of late to walk the streets by night and to haunt strange taverns such as this same Fircone. I am plagued with a womanish curiosity, Tristan, and I thought I would peep over Messire Thibaut's shoulder and have an eye on his cards."

Tristan chuckled. "The Grand Constable bears you a grudge since you chose to turn a kind eye on the girl of Vaucelles."

"She was a wise virgin to dislike Thibaut," mused the king. "Was she a foolish virgin to mistrust your majesty?" questioned Tristan. Louis shrugged his shoulders. "She is a proud piece, gossip. When I told her that she took my fancy she flamed into a red rage that chastened me. But if she's not for me she's not for Thibaut either." "The Grand Constable is a bad enemy," Tristan commented. The king replied at random.

"Tristan, I had a strange dream last night I dreamed that I was a swine rooting in the streets of Paris, and that I found a pearl of great price in the kennel. I picked it up and set it in my crown - "

"A crowned pig," Tristan interrupted. "'Tis like a tavern sign." Louis did not seem to resent the interruption.

"My good gossip, in a dream nothing seems strange. Well, as I said, I set this pearl in my crown and the light of it seemed to fill all my good city of Paris with glory so that I could see every street and alley, every tower and pinnacle, more clearly than in a summer's noon. And then memought that the pearl weighed so heavy upon my forehead that I plucked it from its place and cast it to the ground, and would have trodden it under foot when a star shot swiftly from Heaven and stayed me."

The king looked eagerly at his companion, who seemed wholly uninterested in the narrative of the royal vision. "Dreams and stars, stars and dreams," he sneered. "Leave dreams to weaklings, sire." Louis frowned. "Don't sneer, gossip, but instruct, who are these people?" and the sharp, lean face of the king thrust itself forward a little, bird-like from the nest of its hood, in the direction of the gamblers. His companion shrugged his shoulders.

"Some of the worst cats and rats in all Paris," he answered. "The men belong to a fellowship that is called the Company of the Cockleshells, and babble a cant of their own that baffles the thief-takers. If your majesty - " but here a warning kick from Louis made him wince and change his words-"if you wished to savour rascality these are your blades. The women are trulls. Yonder she-thing in the man's habit is Huguette du Hamel, a wild wench, whom men call the Abbess for her nunnery of light o' loves. There be four of her minions with her now, Jehanneton la belle Heaulmiere as they name her, Denise the slipper-maker, Blanche and Isabeau. Oh, they are delectable doxies!"

King Louis pursed his thin lips in austere censure. "They shall be reproved hereafter," he said. "Who are the men?"

"Worthy Adams of such pestilent Eves," Tristan answered. "That slender fellow in the purple jerkin is one René de Montigny, of gentle birth, and a great breaker of commandments. He with the red hair is Guy Tabarie; they are sworn brothers in bawdry and larceny. The ferret-faced knave who is tickling the girl's knee is Jehan le Loup. Bullies and bawds, pandars and parasites: to enumerate their offenses would be to say the Decalogue backward."

"You have a pithy humour, gossip," and Louis grinned. "Our gallows shall be busy anon."

Tristan was abcut to open his mouth in approval of a sentiment so pleasing to his ears when his words and his purpose were alike arrested by a sound of a voice singing outside the tavern door.

The voice was a man's voice, something rough and strained for fine music, and yet with a kind of full and florid sweetness that carried the words clearly through the red-curtained windows. They seemed to make a complaint of Fortune:

> "Since I have left the prison gate
>   Where I came near to say good-bye
> To this poor life that needs must fly
>   From the malignity of Fate,
> Perchance she now will pass me by
>   Since I have left the prison gate."

If the king pricked his ear to listen, and even Tristan moved a little in his lethargy, the effect of the song upon the company of gamblers was instant and pronounced. The Abbess leaped to her feet, crying out: "It is the voice of François!" "It is indeed his own unutterable pipe," agreed René de Montigny, sweeping his winnings into his pouch. Robin Turgis raised his hands in a comical despair as he muttered: "Here is the devil out of hell again." All the men and women were looking eagerly at the door.

"Who is this?" asked Louis of Tristan, "whose coming seems so to flutter these night-birds?"

"The strangest knave in all Paris," Tristan answered. "One François Villon, scholar, poet, drinker, sworder, drabber, blabber, good at pen, point, and pitcher. In the Court of Miracles they call him the King of the Cockleshells. Judge him for yourself."

CHAPTER II

MASTER FRANÇOIS VILLON

As Tristan spoke the tavern latch rattled, the tavern door was flung noisily open, and the king's gaze rested on a strange figure framed in the entry. The man was of middle height, spare and slight and lean; his thin, eager face was bronzed with the suns and winds of a generation, and lined with the stern ciphers of malign experiences. His dark, straight hair was long and unkempt; the finer lines of his cheeks and chin were blurred with the uncropped growth of a week-old beard; his eyes were bright and quick; his glance restless and comprehensive. A cunning reader of features would have found a home for high thoughts behind the fine forehead, the lines of infinite tenderness upon the mobile lips, the light of some noble conflagration in the wild eyes. He was dressed in faded finery of many colours, so ragged and patched and hostile that he had very much the air of a gaudy scarecrow. His ruined cloak was tilted by a long sword; his disordered thatch was crowned by a battered cap grotesquely adorned with a cock's feather. In his leathern belt a small vellum bound book of verses kept company with a dagger. For all his whimsical appearance the king's keen eyes could note a something gallant in the carriage of the scamp, could spy out qualities of manhood beneath the battered bravery. He poised for a moment on the threshold in a fantastic attitude of salutation ere he slammed the door behind him and strode forward to meet his friends.

"Well, Hearts of Gold, how are ye?" he cried joyously as he advanced with head thrown back and open hands extended. "Did ye miss me, lads; did ye miss me, lasses?"

Abbess Huguette was at his side in an instant, with her arms about his neck fondling him and fawning upon him. "Surely I missed you," she whispered. "Where have you been, little monkey?"

Master François looked at her for a moment with a curious pity. Then gently extricating himself from her embrace he called out, "Give me a wash of wine for my throat's parched with piping."

Every man thrust his own mug towards Master François, beseeching him to drink of it, but he waved them all aside imperially. "Nay, I will have my own," he said. "Have we no landlord here? Master Robin, come hither."

Robin Turgis, who had kept apart up to now, surveying the new-comer with no excess of favour, moved slowly forward with his thumbs in his girdle and a sour smile on his fat cheeks. Master François addressed him sternly, twitching as he did so the landlord's greasy cap from his pate and sending it flying down the room. "Why do you not salute gentry when they honour your pot-house? A mug of your best Beaune, Master Beggar-maker, to drink damnation to the Burgundians."

Robin Turgis made no motion to obey, but his small eyes seemed to grow smaller as they stared. "What colour has money now-a-days, Master François?" he asked doggedly. In a moment the brown, dirty hand of the poet was clapped to his dagger and there was something of a wolfish snarl in his voice as he answered menacingly, "The colour of blood some-times." But the landlord, unabashed and undismayed, stood his ground.

"None of your swaggering, Master François," he said sturdily. "There is such a thing as a king in France and that king's name is writ fair on his coinage. Show me a Louis XI. and I will show you my Beaune wine."

The face of Master François flushed under its grime, and he fiddled at his dagger nervously, as one uncertain whether to laugh or cry at the dilemma which confronted him. Huguette and Montigny alike had dipped their hands into their pouches for money to pay the poet's score when to the amazement of Tristan the king forestalled their kindnesses. Rising to his feet with creditable alacrity he advanced towards Master François and saluted him with a gracious wave of the hand. "Will you let me be of some small service to you," he began politely, and as Villon turned to stare at him in surprise he continued: "Will you honour me by drinking that Beaune wine our host brags of at my expense?"

Villon's astonishment had not unnerved his clutch at opportunity. Here was a god out of a machine, proffering cool liquor to dry gullets. Master François gave back the salutation with a mien of splendid condescension, while the rest of the company glared at the burgess who thus thrust himself upon them, and

Tristan, cursing the king for his temerity, felt for a hidden dagger.

Villon's patronizing wave of the hand was magnificent in its effrontery, and his words matched his gesture nobly.

"You are a civil stranger, and I will so far honour you." Louis bowed. "I left my purse under my pillow this morning" - a roar of laughter saluted the ancient jape - "and this ungentle fellow denies me credit. How rarely we meet with an ale-draper who is also a gentleman."

With an unmoved countenance Louis listened to Villon's words. "Yet the sale of a thing so noble ought to beget a kind of nobility in the vendor," he said with great gravity; then turning to Robin Turgis, whose mouth was gaping at this colloquy, he bade him bring a flagon of his best, and as he did so he tendered him a silver coin for which Robin extended his fat fingers - and extended them too late. For at the sight of the silver the eyes of Master François had glistened, and his lean, brown hand, swift and agile as a hawk, had swooped between the king and the publican, and had secured the coin, which he promptly held up and surveyed in an apparent ecstasy of admiration.

"Is this the good king's counter?" he asked, and as he did so he plucked off his shabby bonnet and paid the exalted coin a profound obeisance. "Well, God bless his majesty, say I, for I owe him my present liberty. There was a gaol-clearing when he came to Paris, and as I happened to be in gaol at the time - through an error of the law" - here he paused to leer knowingly at his comrades, who yelled commendation - "they were good enough to kick me into the free air. Will you add to your kindness, old gentleman" - and here Master François spun round and solemnly saluted his unknown entertainer - "by allowing me to guard and cherish this token of our dear monarch in memory of this notable event?"

Louis' fortitude could not prevent him from making something of a wry face as he hastily answered, "By all means." He beckoned discreetly to Robin Turgis, who, making a wide circle round Master François, stole to the king's side, received from him another coin and hastened away to bring the drink it paid for.

From his corner Tristan surveyed the episode with a grim enjoyment. "Master Villon, Master Villon," he murmured to himself, "you'll be sorry for this, very sorry indeed." And in his mind's eye he transferred the fantastic figure, posturing and grimacing before Louis, to the end of a long rope hanging from a high gallows. Master François, ignorant of the immediate irony of existence, wafted a kiss airily from the tips of his fingers to his patron. "You are a very obliging old gentleman," he said approvingly.

Louis frowned slightly. "You harp on my age, sir," he said. "Yet you are yourself no chicken." This mild reproof seemed to irritate Villon's friends more than it irritated Villon. The men manifested a marked inclination to hustle so questioning a citizen; the women cackled at him angrily. Casin Cholet bluntly proposed to lend the cit a slap on the chops; and Huguette enquired with every emphasis of impoliteness: "What's his age to you, sobersides?" But Villon quietly waved his turbulent companions into tranquility. "Patience, damsels," he said blandly. "Patience, good comrades of the Cockleshell. If our friend is inquisitive at least he has paid his fee," and as he spoke he hid his face for a moment behind the huge mug of Beaune wine which Robin Turgis at that moment handed to him. Much refreshed by his mighty draught he resumed briskly: "For three and thirty years I have taken toll of life with such result as you see. A light pocket is a plague, but a light heart and a light love make amends for much." And as he spoke he slapped his pocket whose emptiness gave back no jingle, drummed lightly on his bosom and nodded gallantly to the admiring womenkind. "You are a philosopher," said the king. "You are a little angel," cried the Abbess, flinging her arms round the poet in an enthusiastic hug. The girl's homage seemed little to Villon's taste, for he disengaged himself swiftly from the embrace, saying as he did so: "Gently, Abbess, gently! My shoulders tingle and my sides ache too sorely for claspings."

Villon's manner was so decisive and his meaning so obvious that the curiosity of the gang burned keenly and found voice in René de Montigny, who asked what ailed him with commendable solicitude. Villon shook his head, applied himself again to the cannakin, and emerged from it with a most melancholy expression of countenance. "You behold in me, friends," he sighed, "a victim of love," and his visage showed so lugubrious that it sorely tempted Louis to laugh, and hotly moved Huguette to anger, for she raged up to Villon, challenging the meaning of his speech. Villon gently cooled her impatience. "Hush, hush, my girl! There are many kinds of love, as you ought to know well enough. I am a rogue and a vagabond, no less, and so sometimes I love you and other such Athanasian wenches; Isabeau there and Jehanneton."

At this mention of her novices' names the Abbess

turned on the two girls fiercely. "You minxes," she cried. "Do you make eyes at my man?" The pair shrank back from her fury, but Master Villon, who seemed suddenly to have fallen into a meditative mood, rambled on in a, kind of reverie, as indifferent to the Fircone and all his surroundings as if he were a lonely shepherd tending his sheep on a lonely hillside.

"But also I am, Heaven forgive me, a jingler of rhymes, with the stars for my candles and the roses for my toys, and singers of songs sometimes love in another fashion. And so it has chanced to me for my sins and to my sorrow."

Villon's chin had dropped upon his breast; the cock's feather drooped dismally; the singer seemed quite chapfallen. Huguette, tired of glaring at her offending minions, again turned her scornful attention to her dejected lover. "Cry-baby!" she sneered scornfully, pointing with derisive finger at Master François, in whose eyes indeed the close observer could discern the threatening of tears. Jehanneton came sidling round to Villon, piqued by natural curiosity, and the desire to vex Huguette. "Tell us your love-tale, François," she pleaded, and her pleading found an immediate supporter in Louis. The Arabian nature of his adventure enchanted him, and he had a child's taste for a story. "May I support the lady's prayer," he said, "unless a stranger's presence distresses you?"

Villon turned to him with a mocking laugh. "Lord love you, no," he answered. "I have long since forgotten reticence and will discourse of my empty purse, my empty belly, and my empty heart to any man. Gather around me, cullions and cut-purses, and listen to the strange adventure of Master François Villon, clerk of Paris."

Joyous applause greeted his speech, Jehan le Loup, seizing upon an empty barrel that stood in a corner, trundled it forward, and standing it on one end invited Villon to take his seat upon this whimsical throne. The poet sprang lightly upon the perch thus provided for him, and sat there with his legs crossed, holding his long sword against his knees with both hands. The men and women gathered about him, like bees about a rose-bush. Huguette placed herself on a stool at his feet. Jehanneton flung herself full length on the ground and stared up into his face. Robin Turgis straddled a bench at some distance and grinned. Louis seized the opportunity to whisper behind his hand to Tristan that he found the fellow diverting, to which Tristan replied gruffly that he for his part found him a dull ape. Louis might have argued the point but his interest was claimed by the voice of Villon, who, being comfortably installed on his wine-cask, was beginning his promised narrative. A philosopher would have discerned something pathetic in the picture of the ragged rascal thus girdled about with blackguards of a baser sort, his lean body quivering, his eager face alive with emotions, mockery on his lips and sorrow in his eyes: to the sardonic king it afforded nothing more and nothing less than amusement. "You must know, dear Devils and ever-beautiful Blowens, that three days ago, when I was lying in the kennel, which is my humour, and staring at the sky, which is my recreation - I speak, honest citizen, but in parable or allegory, a dear device with the schoolmen - I saw between me and Heaven the face of a lady, the loveliest face I ever saw."

Here the poor Abbess, indignation overcrowding her borrowed mannishness, began to sniffle and to assert that the speaker was a faithless pig, but Villon, unheeding her whimpers, went on with his tale.

"She was going to church - God shield her - but she looked my way as she passed, and though she saw me no more than she saw the cobble-stone I stood on, I saw her once and for ever. We song-chandlers babble a deal of love, but for the most part we know little or nothing about it, and when it comes it knocks us silly. I was knocked so silly that - well, what do you think was the silly thing I did?"

Villon turned his alert face to each member of his audience, and his derisive mouth belied the sadness of his eyes.

"Emptied a can for oblivion," Montigny suggested. Blanche was no less practical.

"Kissed a wench for the same purpose," she cried. "The times that I've been wooed out of my name!"

"Picked the woman's pocket," Casin Cholet hinted, wagging his shock head wisely, while Jehan le Loup, with a hideous leer, sniggered: "Got near her in the crowd and pinched her," and suited the action to the word with finger and thumb on Blanche's plump shoulder.

Master François dissipated all this roguish philosophy with a contemptuous gesture.

"La, la, la," he chirruped. "Sillier than all these. I followed her into the church."

The silence of astonishment fell upon the audience.

Justin Huntly McCarthy

Only Colin de Cayeulx had sufficient presence of mind to formulate his amazement in a prolonged whistle. Louis crossed himself repeatedly under his gown. "You are not a church-goer, sir?" he questioned sourly. Villon answered him sweetly.

"No, old Queernabs, unless there's an alms-box to open or a matter of gold plate to pilfer." Guy Tabarie hurriedly interrupted him with a warning cry of "Cave!" and a significant glance at the strangers, but Villon derided his fears.

"Nonsense," he cried, leaning forward and playfully slapping Louis on the back with his sword. "This good Cuffin has a friendly face and can take a joke. Can't you, old rabbit?"

Louis winced and then grinned as Tristan gasped in anger. "I thank Heaven I have a sense ot humour," he said, with a sly glance at his companion. Villon went on with his story.

"Well, I sprawled there in the dark, with my knees on the cold ground, and all the while the sound of her beauty was sweet in my ears, and the taste of her beauty was salt on my lips, and the pain of her beauty was gnawing at my heart, and I prayed that I might see her again."

At this point Huguette, who had been following the narrative with a feline ferocity, caught up a wine-jug and made to throw it at the poet's head, but was dexterously disarmed by Guy Tabarie before the vessel had time to quit her fingers. Sulkily she plumped herself down on her stool again, while Villon, quite unconscious of the averted peril, rambled on dreamily.

"And the incense tickled my nostrils and the painted saints sneered at me, and bits of rhymes and bits of prayers jigged in my brain and I felt as if I were drunk with some new and delectable liquor. And then she slipped out and I after her. She took the Holy Water from my fingers."

Villon's voice sank reverently and Huguette took advantage of the pause.

"I wish it had burned you to the bone," she interrupted spitefully. Master Villon shook his head.

"It burned deeper than that, believe me. Outside, on God's steps, stood a yellow-haired, pink-faced puppet who greeted her and they ambled away together, I on their heels. Presently they came to a gateway and in slips my quarry, and as she did so she turned to her squire and I saw her face again and lost it, for the tears came into my eyes." With a heavy sigh he turned to Louis. "I suppose you wonder why I talk like this, but when my heart's in my mouth I must spit it out or it chokes me."

"I have learned to wonder at nothing," Louis answered sagely. Villon picked up the dropped thread of his tale.

"I saluted the gallant and begged to know the lady's name. He took me for a madman, but he told me."

In a second Huguette was on her legs again and nestling her eager face close to that of Villon as she whispered coaxingly:

"What was the lady's name, dear François?"

Master François looked into her watchful eyes with a wise smile.

"Be secret, sweet," he murmured. "It was Her Majesty, the Queen." A wild roar of laughter from Villon's friends greeted this sally, and the fury it brought to Huguette's face. Louis, royally angered, made as if to rise in protest, but the heavy hand of Tristan fell on his shoulder and restrained him, and Villon, noticing his irritation, waved him down with a pacifying gesture.

"Now, now, my rum duke," he cried, "your loyalty need not take fire. It was not her majesty, but her name I shall keep to myself, though it is written on my shoulders in fair large blue and black bruises."

This statement stirred a murmur of surprise in the gathering. "Did the pink and gold popinjay beat you?" Montigny asked, interpreting the general curiosity.

"No, no," Villon answered. "It came about thus. We tinkers of verses set a price on our wares that few find them worth, yet with the love-fever in my veins I wrote rhymes to this lady and sent them to her fairly writ on a piece of parchment that cost me a dinner."

"Did you think she would come to your whistle like a bird to a lure?" Louis enquired playfully. Villon sighed again.

"In this kind of madness a minstrel thinks himself a new Orpheus who could win a woman out of hell with his music. But I got my answer - oh, I got my answer."

He dropped suddenly into a moody silence, which was not to the taste of the fellowship who were interested in the adventure. Montigny, leaning forward, gave Villon a clap on the back which made him shrink, and shouted "What was the answer?"

Villon began to laugh, a loud, mirthless laugh that had no human warmth in it.

"A fellow like a page boarded me here three days ago. He asked me if I had sent certain verses to a certain quarter. If so I was to follow him at once. I followed like a sheep with my heart drumming till we came to a quiet place, and there four boobies with yard-long cudgels fell upon me. I was taken unawares, I had no weapon but my jackdagger, the blows were raining upon me as fast as acorns fly in a high wind, so I thought it no shame to take to my heels. The varlets pursued me, full cry, till I led them to a part of Paris where their lives would not have been worth a minute's purchase and they had to stay their chase. But I have been rarely drubbed and roundly basted, and my poor back and sides are most womanishly tender. I go abroad no more without Excalibur." He tapped his sword hilt as he spoke. Huguette glared fiercely up at him. "Will it teach you not to play the fool again?" asked, with a vicious snap of her white teeth.

"It will teach me not to play the fool again," Villon answered sadly. "The mark of the beast is upon me and I shall dream no more dreams." He shook himself as if he were trying to shake away clinging memories and extended his empty can to Montigny, saying: "I'm thirsty again. More liquor."

As Montigny filled up for his leader, Louis commented, "You drink more than is good for your health, sir." Villon rounded on him angrily, with flushed face and shining eyes.

"Mind your own business!" he shouted, and the rest shouted with him applaudingly. "What can a man do but drink when France is going to the devil, with the Burgundians camped in the free fields where I played in childhood, and a nincompoop sits on the throne and lets them besiege his city?" The rascals laughed. Tristan whispered to himself, "You'll be sorry you spoke, Master Villon." The king propounded a problem. "No doubt you could do better than the king if you wore the king's shoes?"

Villon rolled about on his barrel in an ecstasy of entertainment. "If I could not do better than Louis Do-Nothing, Louis Dare-Nothing, having his occasions and advantages, may Huguette there never kiss me again."

His boon companions laughed. Huguette whispered sulkily, "Perhaps she never will."

Isabeau came sidling and bridling up to Louis, wheedling like a cat as she said: "Our François has made a rhyme of it, sir, how he would carry himself if he wore the king's shoes."

Louis was always ready for any kind of gallantry. He put his arms around the girl's slim body and drew her on to his knee. "Has he, indeed, pretty minion?" he said. "May we not hear it, Master Poet?"

Villon, with mock modesty, had tried to restrain Isabeau from speaking of the work, but now he changed his tune. "You may; you shall; for 'tis a true song, though it would cost me my neck if it came to the king's ears, very likely. But you are not tall enough to whisper in them, so here goes."

With a shout Villon sprang to his feet, draped his tattered cloak closely about him, struck a commanding attitude, and began to recite with great solemnity. Louis scooped his claw-like fingers behind his ear, that he might hear the better the words that fell from the wild poet's mouth:

> "All French folk, whereso'er ye be,
>   Who love your country, soil and sand.
> From Paris to the Breton sea,
>   And back again to Norman strand,
> Forsooth ye seem a silly band,
>   Sheep without shepherd, left to chance -
> Far otherwise our Fatherland
>   If Villon were the King of France!"

Louis glanced grimly at Tristan; the rogues rubbed their hands and chuckled. Villon smiled in pride and went on:

> "The figure on the throne you see
>   Is nothing but a puppet, planned
> To wear the regal bravery
>   Of silken coat and gilded wand.
> Not so we Frenchmen understand
>   The Lord of lion's heart and glance,
> And such a one would take command
>   If Villon were the King of France!"

The king's face was a study in sardonics. Tristan was poppy-red with rage. The gang applauded and Villon glowed with their applause.

"His counsellors are rogues, Perdie!
   While men of honest mind are banned.
To creak upon the Gallows Tree,
   Or squeal in prisons over-mann'd;
We want a chief to bear the brand,
   And bid the damned Burgundians dance;
God! Where the Oriflamme should stand
   If Villon were the King of France!"

Mugs and cans clattered approval. The rhymer's eyes widened as he drew breath to blow forth the envoi of his ballade.

"Louis the Little, play the grand;
   Buffet the foe with sword and lance;
'Tis what would happen, by this hand,
   If Villon were the King of France!"

A roar of enthusiasm came from the full throats of the band. Montigny slapped Villon on the back with a "Well crowed, Chanticleer!" Huguette flung her arms around him and hugged him as she cried passionately: "I forgive you much, for that light in your eyes."

But the poet seemed weary after so much heat. He pushed the girl away and drooped on his hogshead. The rogues rattled away to their table again, and Villon was left alone with Louis, who questioned him drily: "You call yourself a patriot, I suppose?"

Villon had recovered sufficient energy to drain a mug of wine. He turned to the king, passing his hand over his forehead. "By no such high-sounding title," he answered. "I am but a poor devil with a heart too big for his body and a hope too large for his hoop. Had I been begotten in a brocaded bed, I might have led armies and served France; have loved ladies without fear of cudgellings, and told kings truths without dread of the halter, while as it is, I consort with sharps and wantons, and make my complaint to a dull little buzzard like you, old noodle! Oh,'tis a fool's play and it were well to be out of it."

"You won't have long to worry," Tristan muttered to himself under his breath, and found great comfort in the thought. Louis merely said: "You are sententious!"

Villon took him up swiftly. "The quintessence of envy, no less. I have great thoughts, great desires, great ambitions, great appetites, what you will. I might have changed the world and left a memory. As it is I sleep in a garret under the shadow of the gallows, and shall be forgotten to-morrow, even by the wolves I pack with. But this is dry thinking; let's to drinking!" As he spoke Villon rose to join his comrades, when his quick eye noted that Robin Turgis had fallen asleep on his bench. Villon skipped lightly toward him, dexterously unhooked his bunch of keys from his girdle, and, with a triumphant gesture, made on tiptoe for the cellar door, which he unlocked and through which he disappeared. Louis looked after him with an acid smile. Tristan leaned forward and plucked at the kind's sleeve. "Shall I hang him to-morrow?" he asked, hoarsely. The king turned, musing, to his henchman. "We shall see! He is a loose-lipped fellow, but he might have been a man. He has set me thinking of my dream. I was a swine rioting in the streets of Paris and I found a pearl-well, well. Let us kill the time with cards till Thibaut d'Aussigny comes." Tristan produced a pack of cards from his pouch and laid them on the table. "Do you think he will come?" he asked.

"He does not expect to find me here, I promise you," Louis answered. "He would not come if he did. Barber Olivier is to warn me of his coming." As he spoke the inn-door opened a little and the king, hearing the click of the catch, asked: "Is that he?"

Tristan glanced round over his shoulder. The door was pushed partly open, and an old, stooped woman was peeping curiously into the room. Tristan shrugged his shoulders.

"No, sire," he snarled, "another old woman."

By this time the king had arranged the cards to his satisfaction. He made an imperative gesture to his companion to seat himself and in a few seconds had forgotten everything else in the excitement of the game. Meanwhile the old woman, having pushed the door wide open, came softly into the room. She was a quiet, mild-faced creature, one of those human shadows who suggest without tragedy faded youth and withered comeliness. She was very poorly but very neatly dressed, in worn grey and rusty black, and the linen folds about her lined face were scrupulously clean. She looked anxiously around her, shading her eyes with her hand, in the dim light of the tavern, unable to discern much but evidently eager to discern something.

René de Montigny, tired of teasing Isabeau, suddenly looked up and caught sight of the old woman as she stood, very helpless and wistful, peering about her. An impish spirit floated leaf-like on the surface of his mind. He rose to his feet and danced towards her in a fantastic manner, sweeping her a profound salutation as he approached her.

"Your pleasure, sweet princess?" he said with mock deference.

The old woman turned her wrinkled visage up to his in wonder.

"Is Master François Villon in this company, sir?" she faltered.

Montigny treated her to another profound bow.

"Sweet creature," he simpered, "I kiss your hand and inquire."

He turned to his companions at the table and his eye rested mockingly on the bowed figure of Huguette. After Master Villon had told his tale Huguette had been glum enough, and her comrades finding her snappish wisely left her to herself. She had pulled a pack of cards from her scarlet pouch; she had been spelling out her fortune silently, and the death card insisted itself again and again with grim pertinacity. With a sense of despair that was strange to her airy nature she had bowed her face on her arms and was sobbing softly to herself. Montigny was not a man to be touched by a woman's sorrow. He mockingly gesticulated over her bent shoulders as he cried to the others in a false whisper,

"There is a beautiful woman at the door, beseeching our François."

The moment these words fell on Huguette's ears, they stung her into life and activity. She leaped to her feet in a flash.

"What do you say?" she raged, and then, seeing a woman's form a few feet away from her, she rushed towards the stranger furiously while the others rose in cages expectation of some new excitement.

"What do you seek here?" she asked fiercely of the old woman, and then as she saw the pitiful wrinkled face staring up at her, she started back in surprise.

The old woman, misinterpreting the sex of her questioner from the dress that Huguette wore, began apologetically.

"Asking your pardon, young gentleman," and for a moment her words were drowned in a shout of delighted laughter, as the listening rogues appreciated the blunder she had made.

"Asking your pardon, young gentleman, I seek Master François Villon."

Huguette snapped at her impatiently, "Seek him and find him." Then turning to René, she cried, "Montigny, you beast!" and with her hand on her dagger, made hotly for him.

Montigny, grinning like a delighted monkey, skipped for safety, dodging her around the table, while the others perceiving a victim in the bewildered old woman, joined hands in a ring and began dancing wildly around her, singing a ribald song. The old woman, as frightened and timid as a mouse might be if it suddenly found itself the centre of a circle of dancing cats, stood still.

At this moment the cellar door opened, and François

reappeared, carrying in his arms a large jug of wine. Perceiving that the landlord still lay in his heavy sleep, he smiled delightedly to himself, closed the cellar door softly and placed his booty in the corner of the fireplace nearest to the settle. The noise of the tumult attracted him from his successful plunder, and looking up, he became aware of what was happening. In a second his contented mien changed, and dashing into the dancing crowd, he struck Jehan le Loup a heavy blow with the bunch of keys, which felled him to the ground like a log. In a moment the cluster of rascals dissipated, and Villon caught the old woman in his arms.

"Damn you, chubs!" he shouted at them. "It's my mother." Then as he drew the trembling old woman towards the fireplace, he whispered in her ears, "Don't be frightened, mammy, they meant no harm."

A certain hang-dog air of contrition was on the faces of most of the members of the gang as they stood apart and eyed the mother and son shame-facedly. Guy Tabarie, who had a wholesome dislike to quarrels, slipped quietly into the cool street to seek pleasure in some place where the atmosphere might be less stormy.

Robin Turgis wakened from his heavy sleep, clapped his hand instinctively to his girdle and found that his keys were missing.

"My keys! my keys!" he shouted - "where are my keys?" And then, catching sight of them where they lay by the prostrate form of Jehan le Loup, he rushed forward and secured them greedily.

By this time Jehan le Loup had recovered the senses which Villon's swinging blow had knocked out of him and was crawling slowly into a sitting posture. He glared ferociously at Master François and his evil right hand stole to the pommel of his dagger.

"You have cracked my crown, curse you," he grunted, and then swiftly sprang to his feet with the bare blade in his hand and rushed at his assailant. But Villon was too alert to be taken unawares. He had not time to draw his sword, but in a second he had snatched a spit from the fire and extending it scientifically kept Jehan le Loup at arm's length. Huguette seized Jehan by the dagger arm.

"She is his mother!" she said angrily. "You all had mothers, I suppose? Let him alone!"

Jehan le Loup unwillingly sheathed his weapon; Huguette dragged him back to the table; Villon replaced the spit, which had somewhat burned his fingers, and sat down by his mother's side on the settle, in peace.

"Did they frighten you, mammy?" he whispered. "But they meant no harm. Boys and girls, girls and boys."

The old woman put her arms tightly about him. Villon grimaced. Her loving touch was as painful as a hostile one to his bruised body, but he made no attempt to repress her embrace.

"Come home, François," she said. "Come home. Where have you been these three days?"

Villon caressed the old woman very tenderly, as

he answered:

"Very busy, mammy - state secrets. Mum's the word. How did you find me out?"

"They told me at the Unicorn," the old woman said, "that I might find you here."

Villon made a gesture of contempt.

"Oh, the Unicorn is no longer fashionable. They want payment on the nail there, confound them! Besides, this is nearer the walls and we can hear the Burgundians shouting. It is as good as a relish with our wine."

Mother Villon shook her grey head sadly.

"Come away," she entreated. "You have had wine enough."

Villon contradicted her instantly.

"Never in my life, mammy. I have a fool's head and always get into my altitudes too soon."

Then, seeing the look of disappointment that made her grey old face look greyer still, - he added, "I cannot come home just now, mammy, but there is something I can do for you. Do you remember when I was a little child - "

Something in the words made him stop suddenly. The hideous contrast between the phrase and the place wherein he was, between the mother who fondled him and the wild men-savages and women-savages who were his daily friends and who were drinking and dicing behind him at the other side of the settle, came upon him like a great wave of pain and knocked the mirth out of him. He turned away from his mother and repeated to himself dismally, "God! when I was a little child!" The mother's pity, the mother's protection immediately asserted themselves.

"You were the prettiest child woman ever bore," she said, softly.

Villon turned towards her again, while he tried to wink the tears out of his eyes.

"You used to sing me to sleep," he said, and as he spoke he rocked her slowly backward and forward in his arms, while he crooned the words of that old nurse's song which has soothed so many generations of French children to sleep, "Do, do, l'enfant do, l'enfant dormira tantot."

"Well, mammy, your dutiful son has made a song for you to sing yourself to sleep with. I went to church the other day. Oh, on my honour, I did" - this was in reply to a startled look of surprise that flooded the old woman's face - "and a prayer came into my head - a prayer for you to say to our Lady."

The old woman kissed him fondly on the forehead.

"My love bird," she said, and as she spoke a boyish look that had long been absent from Villon's face came back to it for a moment.

"Here it is," he said. "Listen." And he whispered to her the verses he had made, while the old woman crossed herself reverentially.

> "Lady of Heaven, Queen of Earth,
> Empress of Hell, I kneel and plead
> You pity, by the holy birth,
> The humblest Christian of the Creed;
> I cannot write; I cannot read;
> I am a woman poor and old,
> But in the Church, where I behold
> The gates of Paradise, I cry
> Woman to woman, make me bold
> In thy belief to live and die."

"There, mammy, there is a pretty prayer for you."

Mother Villon was dissolved in tears and sobbed on his shoulder.

"You should have been a good man," she said.

Villon stroked her hair very gently.

"We are as Heaven pleases, dear." He paused for a moment, then suddenly remembering the silver coin which he had confiscated from the king, he dipped his fingers into his pouch and produced it.

"Here is something for you, mammy," he said, and as the old woman, with a faint flush on her worn cheeks, seemed about to protest, he insisted. "Oh, yes. Take it, take it. It was honestly come by, and you will spend it more honestly than I should." He forced the coin into her lean, brown hand, and added, "Now run away, mammy, and pray yourself to sleep, You shall see me soon, I promise you."

He led her gently across the tavern floor to the door, which he opened for her. As she turned to go, she looked up to him and repeated two lines of his prayer:

"Woman to woman, make me bold In thy belief to live and die."

As the door closed and Villon turned to come back to his seat, Jehan le Loup, who had been eyeing him and who was eager to pay off the score of his cracked crown, rose to his feet, dragging Isabeau with him, and barred his passage.

"Kiss a young mouth for a change," he said, and thrust the girl against the poet. Villon brushed them both aside.

"Go to the devil," he said angrily, and passed them. Once again Jehan's hand sought his weapon and once again he was restrained.

"He is in one of his bad moods," said Isabeau. "Leave him to himself," and she drew her reluctant companion back to the table, while Villon seated himself in a corner of the settle, staring into the fire.

At the moment the tavern door was thrust open violently and Guy Tabarie rushed into the room, his great moon face sweating, his eyes bulging, his fringe of crimson locks flaming out from the eggshell dome of his bald head, his mighty belly swaying with a passion of excitement.

"Friends!" he shrieked, at the top of his voice, "there's a fight at Fat Margot's between two wenches. They are stripped to the waist and at it hammer and tongs. Come and see for the love of God!"

The whole band was afoot in an instant, clamantly agog. Guy Tabarie turned as he finished speaking and rushed through the open door into the shining moonlit street. The rest trailed after him, wandering stars in the tail of a dishonourable comet, shouting, screaming, laughing, pushing, panting, eager for the promised sport.

"I'll crown the victor!" cried Montigny as he ran and "I'll console the vanquished!" shouted Jehan le Loup, as he brought up the rear of the road and vanished, clattering, into the night. Only Huguette remained of all the fellowship, and she turned instinctively to Villon when he crouched over the dying fire.

"Will you come, François?" she whispered softly. Villon lifted his head for a moment from his hands to signify a refusal.

"Nay, I am reading."

Huguette blazed out at him a fierce "You lie!" which failed to move the poet from his melancholy resolve.

"A man may read without book," he said. "Go your ways, girl, and skelp both the hussies!" He drooped into a dejected heap again, oblivious of the girl, who looked at him half sadly, half angrily for an instant, and then disappeared in her turn into the causeway, calling upon her knavish heralds to wait for her.

Robin Turgis, shutting the door after her with a sigh of satisfaction, retired to his own quarters to seek sleep until custom should return. Louie and Tristan, deep in their cards, paid little heed to anything else.

"Your barber tarries," Tristan said, after a panse.

"The game makes amends," Louis answered.

"You are winning, sire," Tristan grunted. The king chirruped merrily.

"My grandsire will be remembered longer than most kings for the sake of these wasters and winners that they made to soothe his madness."

But even as he spoke his mirth faded, for a turn of Fortune gave Tristan an opportunity.

"My game, sire!" he said, and swept the stakes into his pocket.

The king fell into a frowning silence as Tristan dealt the cards again, and scrutinized his new hand with a sombre care, as if the fate of Empire depended upon it. Scarcely a sound disturbed the heavy quiet of the room. Master François Villon glooming in his settle corner, sucked a long noiseless draught from his stolen jug and meditated drearily. Between wine and weariness his head was beginning to swim. His head felt as heavy as lead and his brain as light and foolish as a wind-tumbled feather. Two women's faces danced before his eyes, one proud and beautiful and young, the other humble and pitiful and old, and he tried his best to shut both of them out of his senses. Vaguely he tried to shape a ballade, a noble ballade in honour of all things good to eat. He had got at least an excellent overword. "A dish of tripe's the best of all." He mouthed the line with a relish, but his eyes were seeing straws and his stubbled chin scraped his breast. There came a click at the latch, but he did not heed it. He would scarcely have heeded a Burgundian cannon shot; he had drifted into a lumpish doze. And yet the way of the world depended, for him, upon that lift of a latch.

CHAPTER III

THE COMING OF KATHERINE

The door opened and a woman entered the room, a woman closely muffled after the fashion adopted by discreet ladies when they walked abroad in Paris in the fifteenth century. She was followed by an armed serving-man to whom she turned and spoke in a whisper as she paused upon the threshold.

"You are sure this is the place?" she asked, and the man answered -

"Sure!"

"Wait outside!" the muffled lady commanded, and the servant with an obeisance stepped back into the street. The woman looked cautiously about her, only her bright eye showing over the lifted fold of her cloak. Villon was hidden from her while he sat; there was no one in her view save the two men playing cards. She came cautiously forward and touched Tristan, who was nearest to her, on the shoulder. He swung round, with hooded face, to answer the challenge, and as he did so Louis took advantage of his turned back to examine Tristan's hand, which he had laid upon the table, and to substitute a card from his own hand for one of his adversary's.

"Has Master François Villon been here to-night?" the woman asked. Her voice was full and sweet, and Tristan knew it well though he listened unmovably. She had lowered her cloak enough to allow him a glimpse of a young, lovely face, but he needed no, glimpse to assure him.

"Yonder he squats by the hearth," he answered, masking his own voice with hoarseness and jerking his thumb towards the settle. The girl's eyes followed the signal and saw for the first time the huddled figure on the bench. "I thank you," she said simply, and moved away into the background, her eyes fixed on the crouching form, her fingers clasped nervously, waiting an impatient patience upon resolution.

Tristan leaned hurriedly over to the king.

"Zounds, sire! do you know who that was?"

Louis, smiling at his adopted cards, answered carelessly, "Some bonaroba who took you for a gull," but Tristan's nest words pricked him from his indifference.

"It was your majesty's kinswoman, the Lady Katherine de Vaucelles."

The king rose cautiously to his feet.

"Oh, ho, Oh, ho!" he chuckled. "Does lovely Katherine come to meet Thibaut?"

"She seeks François Villon, sire."

The king started.

"Is she the girl he spoke of? Do we catch her tripping?"

Louis looked at the motionless figure of the girl, then his gaze travelled rapidly around the room. Behind him was a doorway. Soundlessly he opened it, saw that it gave on to a dark passage, motioned Tristan through it, bade him in a whisper to wait in the darkness. As Tristan disappeared the girl seemed to make up her mind and moved slowly across the floor toward the dozing poet. The king watched her narrowly as he, too, began to move, skulking among the shadows along the wall. His goal was the distant space behind the settle, where his cunning mind discerned a good listening place - for to listen was Louis' passion. The king's cread was cat-quiet - the king's breath was mouse-still; for a moment he paused at the street-door as if about to pass out, but seeing that he was unnoticed he drifted unheeded through obscurity to his haven and nestled there just as the girl, bending forward, touched the sleeper firmly on the shoulders and then drew back, defiantly abiding by her temerity.

Villon moved uneasily, as if resenting the interruption to his slumbers that the firm touch had disturbed, and he grumbled sullenly, without looking up, "What is it?"

The woman bent towards him again and whispered "A word with you."

Villon rose wearily to his feet, and as he did so the woman drew back towards the open centre of the room, which now appeared to her to be empty. Her nerves were too highly strung to note anything surprising in the disappearance of the two visitors. If she thought of them at all it was only to be glad that they had gone their ways and left the place so lonely. Villon followed her almost unconsciously, too sleepy for wonder. Suddenly the woman threw off the folds that muffled her face and the vision that had haunted him flashed on his frightened eyes, the vision so proud, so beautiful and young. He crossed himself as he questioned in a voice that sounded strangely alien to him, "Are you real?"

"Do I look like a ghost?" the fair woman answered.

In an ecstasy of joy Villon fell on his knees as he seldom kneeled in prayer, while he gasped,

"If this be a dream, pray Heaven I may never wake."

The girl drew from her bosom a little piece of folded parchment and held it out towards him.

"You wrote me these verses. My elders tell me that poets say much and mean little; that their oaths are like gingerbread, as hot and sweet in the mouth and as easily swallowed. 'Are you such a one?"

Villon rose to his feet. He knew that this exquisite presence was flesh and biood; that her speech was human speech. He answered her very gravely -

"My words are life. I love you!"

"Just because I show a smooth face?"

A great wave of rapture swept over the poet's soul and his brain seemed as busy with words as a hive with bees. He spoke slowly like a man inspired.

Justin Huntly McCarthy

"Because you are the loveliest she alive. If all my dreams of loveliness had been pieced together into one perfect woman she would have been like you. All my life I have read tales of love and tried to find their secret in the bright eyes about me - tried and failed. I might as well have been seeking for the Holy Grail. But when I saw you the old Heaven and the old Earth seemed to shrivel away and I knew what love might mean, and God-like desire and God-like surrender. The world is changed by; your coming, all sweet tastes and fair colours and soft sounds have something of you in them. I eat and drink, I see and hear in your honour. The people in the street are blessed because you have passed among them. That stone on the ground is sacred, for your foot has touched it; or the dusty booth at the corner, which your sleeve has brushed in passing. I love you! All philosophy, all wisdom, religion, honour, manhood, hope, beauty lie in those words - I love you!"

The girl looked at him with wide eyes, quite fearless, much astonished, as a brave maid might look at some wild beast of the woods that came in her way. But the purport of his words seemed to please her, for she answered him quickly and readily.

"Well, I have come to you to put your protestations to the proof. If you meant every word you said, every syllable, every letter, you can serve me well. If not, good-night and good-bye."

And with these words she moved a little as if she were ready to say farewell to him then and there. Villon put forward an appealing hand that stayed her.

"I wrote with my heart's blood," he protested, and even

a green girl could not fail to read the truth in his voice. Now she came close to him, speaking very low but very distinctly.

"Listen. I am one of the Queen's ladies; Thibaut d'Aussigny, the Grand Constable of France, loves me a little and my broad lands much. He wills that I should marry him. He tried to force me to his will, to shame me to his pleasure, and so I hate him, and so should you, for it was he who gave you your beating."

Villon, who had been listening to her in wonder, started as if he had been struck anew.

"Oh, it was he?" he interrupted. The girl came a little closer, became a little more confidential.

"He gave your rhymes to me and told me how you had been treated. When I read them I said - here, if a poet speaks truth, is the one man in France who can help me."

Villon drew himself back with a little shiver of intelligence. The lumes of wine, the fumes of wonder were drifting away from him, leaving him face to face with naked, amazing reality.

"Why not your yellow-haired, pink-faced lover?" he asked. Katherine frowned disdain.

"Noel le Jolys is a man many women might love, but I love no man; I only hate Thibaut d'Aussigny. Do you understand?"

"I begin to understand," Villon answered, sadly.

The girl came nearer to Villon. Her face was very pale in the dim light, and a fleeting image of the moon in clouds teased his fancy. Her lips were as red, he thought, as the ruby of a bishop's ring, and her eyes out-starred Venus. So it was he who trembled and not the maiden who was saying strange unmaiden-like words in a clear, steel-like whisper.

"Kill Thibaut d'Aussigny. You are a skillful swordsman, they say. You are little better than an outlaw. You say you love me more than life. Kill Thibaut d'Aussigny!"

Villon looked at her queerly. To save his life he could not keep his face from quivering. He was eating his heart and it tasted very bitter, and his own voice sounded far away to him, like a voice heard in a dream.

"So that you and Noel what's his name may live happily ever after?"

Katherine drew back from him, a little scorn in her eyes and on her lips.

"Are you less eager to serve me than you were?"

The question struck him in the breast like the stroke of a sword. He remembered his golden vows and his golden verses, and sickened at his shadow of disloyal doubt and anger.

"No, by Heaven, but I've been dozing and dreaming, and I've got to rub the sleep out of my eyes and the dream out of my heart. Tell me how to serve you."

She was reassured on the instant and neared him again confidently.

"Thibaut d'Aussigny comes here to-night. He has come here before in disguise, for I have had him followed. I think he means to betray the king to Burgundy, so you will serve France as well as me. How do such men as you kill each other?"

Villon looked at her ironically out of the corner of his eyes; answered her ironically out of the corner of his mouth. He saw himself as she saw him, and was sadly entertained at the sight.

"Generally in a drunken scuffle. Will you wait here till he comes, pretty lady, for I never saw him? Then leave the rest to me."

Something in his voice, though it was firm and clear, seemed to touch the girl's ear more than any word he had yet uttered. A new curiosity seemed to lurk in her eyes and there was almost a sound of pity in her speech.

"You love me very much?" she asked softly. Villon drew himself up proudly and answered her proudly.

"With all the meaning that the word can have in Paradise."

A faint shade of colour came into the woman's pale, pure cheeks.

"You didn't expect to be taken at your word?"

Villon smiled brightly and his eyes were dancing,

though his heart was heavy enough.

"I didn't hope to be, I will try to be worthy of the honour."

The girl's eyes shone with wonder.

"You love and laugh in the same breath," she asserted.

Villon made a deprecatory gesture with his hands, half in protest, half in approval.

"That is my philosophy."

This view of life seemed to astonish her not a little. She caught her breath for a moment, then suddenly glided close to him.

"If you wish," she said in an even whisper, "you may kiss me once."

All the blood in the man's heart seemed to turn to fire and flame into his face as he turned towards her, making as if he would take her face in his hands and seal his soul upon her mouth. Then he sharply flung himself away from her.

"Nay, I can fight and if needs must die in your quarrel, but if once I touched your lips - that would make life too sweet to adventure."

The woman's face had flushed a little at her offer: it now paled again.

"As you will," she said, and as she spoke there came the noise of shouting, singing and trampling feet outside. The poet dropped in a moment from the dizzy pinnacle of dreamland to the calm valley of a commonplace world.

"These are my friends returning," he said. "They mustn't see you. Come this way." As he spoke he caught her hand and drew her across the room to the stairs that led to the upper gallery. On the gallery he bade her wait.

"Here you can see without being seen. When he comes, show him to me. Then you can reach the street by this passage."

Even as he spoke the main door was dashed open and the wild rout foamed into the room, bubbling with exhilaration, Huguette leaping like a bubble on the eddies of their enthusiasm. Louis and Tristan took advantage of the confusion to emerge from their hiding places and resume their seats at their table,

"That was rare sport while it lasted," Colin shouted.

"It didn't last long enough," Jehan yelled.

"Things took a different turn when you came, Abbess," Montigny said, patting the girl on the back approvingly. Huguette shook her long hair out of her eyes and laughed as she turned down her rolled-up sleeves.

"I did as François bade me and basted both the jades. Wine, landlord, wine! My arms ache."

Robin Turgis was prompt; flagons and pipkins rattled as the men and women gathered round their table and Renéwed their drinking and dicing with fresh zest from the scuffle they had just witnessed. Guy Tabarie laughed one of his long fat laughs as he lingered over memory's picture of the way Huguette had trussed and trounced each of the amazons. "Lord, how they squeaked and wriggled!" he said unctuously.

Louis whispered to his companion.

"Our mad poet may do me a good turn, Gossip Tristan."

Even as he spoke the inn door opened and a man entered - a small man, plainly clad, with his hood about his face. He glanced about him anxiously till he caught sight of Louis and Tristan, for whom he made immediately. Villon, craning over the balustrade, saw him and touched the girl on the arm to call her attention to the new-comer.

"Is that he?" he whispered. The girl shook her head.

"No, no. Thibaut is a big man. Yet that figure seems familiar."

The stranger came to the table and stooped between Louis and Tristan. Louis looked up and grinned recognition of his barber, Olivier le Dain.

"He is coming, sire," Olivier said.

"You are sure?"

"We dogged his footsteps all the way, till I slipped ahead. Here he comes!"

With finger on lip Olivier glided through the door

behind which Tristan had been concealed a few moments before. The king rubbed his hands and chuckled. Even Tristan looked pleased.

Justin Huntly McCarthy

CHAPTER IV

ENTER THIBAUT

Once again the door swung on its hinges admitting a very tall, powerful man, dressed like a common soldier, his brawny bulk panoplied in steel and leather. He glanced about him as he entered, exchanged looks with René de Montigny and came down to the settle, where he flung his vast body with a clatter while he called to the landlord in a bull's bellow to bring him some wine.

Katherine leaning and looking gave a little gasp. "That is he!" she breathed into Villon's ear. Villon gave an involuntary sigh, partly indeed of satisfaction at the thought that his quarry was before him, a very vast and royal stag for a hunter's hand to threaten, but partly too of exquisite regret. It had been very sweet to crouch there in the darkness of the stairway so close to the one fair woman of all the world, to feel her breath upon his cheek, almost to hear her heart-beats, to know that once if only for once they were alone together and allied in a common purpose, to feel the touch of her soft gown, to know that if he chose he could touch her hair with his outstretched hand. Those seconds of strange intimacy seemed to be worth all the rest of his life - and now they had come to an end. Now he had to show that he deserved them. "Good," he said, and leaving her side he softly descended the stairs, crept cat-foot across the tavern floor and insinuated himself dexterously into the society of his friends, who were by this time far too mad and merry to show any surprise at his sudden re-appearance, or to question whence he came. Only one of the fellowship was away from the board - René de Montigny, who had risen as soon as the soldier had taken his seat by the fireplace, and had come down to greet him in a seemingly careless, off-hand fashion. Villon dexterously moving from friend to friend managed to niche himself by the back of the settle where he could catch some of the words that passed between Montigny and the stranger, whose meeting was also the subject of unsuspected scrutiny on the part of the unassuming burgesses who sat apart and to whom no one now gave heed.

"A fine evening, friend," Montigny said affably.

"Pretty fine for the time of year," the soldier answered. "How is your garden, friend?"

Montigny smiled whimsically.

"Very salubrious, if it were not for the shooting stars."

Then as the soldier stared at him he hastened to explain.

"My quip. The shooting star was a Burgundian arrow a cloth-yard long which came winging its way over the walls at noon and made itself at home in my garden. Here is what the arrow carried."

He pulled from his pouch a small piece of parchment folded and sealed, and handed it to the seeming soldier.

Justin Huntly McCarthy

The disguised constable took the missive and scanned it narrowly.

"The seal has not been tampered with," he said to himself. Ren caught him up with a noble gesture of indignation.

"I never read other people's letters," he protested.

Thibaut shrugged his shoulders.

"It would have profited you little if you had," he said, as he broke the seal and turning aside stooped a little to read by the faint fire light what the letter said. It was couched in words that seemed commonplace enough, but Thibaut knew their secret meaning, knew that the Duke of Burgundy would do all that he asked, give him a duchy, give him the girl he coveted, all that he might ask for or lust for if he would only play the traitor and deliver Louis into the Duke of Burgundy's hands. As this was precisely what Thibaut was resolved to do, a pleased smile played over his lips as he tossed the parchment into the glowing ashes and watched it wither into nothingness. He turned to Montigny, who was watching him attentively.

"Can you command some safe rogues of your kidney who think better of Burgundian gold than of the fool on the throne?"

Montigny answered him behind his hand. "Aye. I know of half a dozen stout lads who would pilfer the king from his palace of the Louvre if they were paid well enough for the job," and he jerked his thumb over his shoulder in the direction of his carousing comrades. Thibaut nodded approval. He thrust some gold into

Montigny's ready palm, whispered to him to meet him again to-morrow, and as Montigny rejoined his friends he turned to leave the tavern.

To his surprise he found himself confronted by Villon, who feigning intoxication barred his passage with an air of great hilarity. "You walk abroad late, honest soldier," he hiccoughed.

"That's my business," Thibaut answered, trying to pass, but Villon still delayed him.

"Don't be testy. Come and crack a bottle."

"I've had enough, and you've had more than enough," Thibaut growled. "Go to bed!"

Villon's false good humour changed in a clap.

"You're a damned uncivil fellow, soldier, and don't know how to treat a gentleman when you see one."

Thibaut began to lose patience.

"Get out of the way!" he said, and gave Villon a little push with his open hand that made him stagger. Villon's voice rose to a yell.

"I will not get out of the way! How do I know you are an honest soldier? How do I know that you are a true man?"

As Villon's voice rose the altercation attracted the attention of the revellers. Montigny glided to Villon's side and whispered him.

"Let him alone, François; he's not what he seems."

"Seems! Who cares what he seems?" Villon shouted. "It's what he is I want to know. Perhaps he's not an honest soldier at all. Perhap's he's a damned Burgundian spy!"

Thibaut lifted his hand to crush Villon, but the poet's naked dagger menaced him and he paused.

"Fling this drunken dog into the street," he commanded angrily. Villon's friends snapped at him furiously. Villon flung back the phrase.

"Drunken dog, indeed! You are a lying, ill-favoured knave! Keep the door, friends, this rogue has insulted me. Pluck out your iron, soldier!"

In a moment the whole pack were between Thibaut and the door, every woman a fury, every man a fighter, every man with the exception of René de Montigny, who, dexterously disentangling himself from the mass of his companions, made for the side door and slipped out of it unheeded in the confusion. It was his intention to alarm the watch and intervene for the protection of his powerful patron, and with this purpose in his mind he disappeared into the darkness of the street and ran as fast as his legs could carry him.

In the meantime the quarrel at the Fircone raged hotter. Thibaut, glaring at his enemies as a bull might glare at barking dogs, asked savagely of the poet who was brandishing his sword:

"Who the devil are you?"

Villon flung has head back defiantly and flourished his sword.

"I am François Villon, and my sword is as good as another man's."

The moment the name fell on Thibaut's ears the giant gave a giant's laugh.

"Are you François Villon?" he thundered. "Lend me a cudgel, some one," and he looked around as if seeking for the weapon he asked for..Villon snatched up a mug and flung the heel taps in the soldier's face, spotting his cheeks with drops of crimson that trickled on to his breast plate. With a choking cry of rage Thibaut dragged his sword into the air.

"You fool," he hissed, "I'll kill you!"

"We shall see," Villon answered gallantly, as he stood on guard alert and wary.

For a moment the he-rascals and she-rascals held their breath. The great figure in the shining steel seemed so to dominate the slight frame of their favourite that anything like an equal contest between the two men seemed little less than ridiculous. What skill of Villon's could hope to avail against the mighty sweep of that huge soldier's weapon? Suddenly the swift spirit of Huguette solved the problem. Springing forward with the delicate agility of a young panther, she poised, opinionative, between the opponents.

"Fair play!" she screamed. "This is David and Goliath," and as she spoke she pointed with one hand at Villon while with the other she struck with her open palm a ringing blow on the cuirass of Villon's antagonist. "Let them fight it out with sword and lantern in the dark."

A loud shout of applause greeted the girl's suggestion. That fantastic form of duello was not unfamiliar to the free companions of the Court of Miracles, and Villon himself, eager as he was for the combat, was keen enough to see how well this way might work for the surety of his purpose. Skill, inches, tricks of fence, all things were equal when men fought as shadows in shadowland.

"What do you say, Goliath?" he laughed, and the grim face of Thibaut smiled responsive.

"As you please," he said, serenely confident in his strength and length of arm. "It is all one to me." Then suddenly looking round on the leering, sullen faces about him, a wolfish girdle of ferocity, he caught back his agreement and held it for a moment. "On this condition," he added. "When there is an end of you, there is an end of the quarrel. Your friends here must agree to that."

Villon agreed on the instant. He was all for ridding the world of Thibaut, but he wanted to do it himself for the sake of the white girl crouching on the stairway.

"I promise," he said, "for myself and for them," and turning to the girl, he insisted, "Promise, Huguette; swear it!"

"I swear it," Huguette answered.

"That is settled," said Villon. "Now, friends, make a

ring and dowse the glim."

In another instant, the preparations for the combat were afoot, Robin Turgis, angrily protesting against the desecration of his orderly hostelry and shouting wild words about summoning the watch, was promptly overpowered by Jehan le Loup, who forced him on to a bench and kept him there with a dagger's point at his throat. The women huddled, screaming and excited, on the stairway a little below the place where Katherine crouched, holding her breath and peeping through the railings. The men stood behind tables and on benches, while Casin Cholet and Colin de Cayeulx dived into the landlord's quarters and reappeared bearing each in his hand a lighted lantern. While these preparations were being hurried toward, Tristan, full of alarm, leaned forward and plucked at the king's mantle.

"This must be put a stop to, sire," he whispered; but the king shook his head with a grim smile of satisfaction.

"On the contrary, gossip," he answered, "whichever of these rascals kills the other, does the state a service and saves the hangman some labour."

Villon crossed the room and came close to where Thibaut waited sullen. "I think I shall square our reckoning, Master Thibaut," he whispered. The giant stared at him. "You know me?" he gasped. "Your varlets thumped me yesterday," Villon answered. "I shall tickle you to-day. Turn, turn about, friend Thibaut."

Even as he spoke Guy Tabarie puffed out the last candle left alight in the room, which was plunged instantly into almost total darkness. Even the faint

Justin Huntly McCarthy

moonlight that had come through the window was swiftly veiled by Huguette, who drew the crimson curtains close together. The dim light from the fire only seemed to accentuate and intensify the darkness through which the two lanterns burned, pale planets of yellow fire, in the hands of Casin and Colin. Villon snatched the one and Thibaut took the other. There was a moment of intense silence; then the voice of Huguette cried out of the blackness: "Are you ready?"

Both combatants cried, "Yes!" in the same breath, and in the next the battle began.

No stranger fight had ever been fought within those walls before, or even perhaps within the walls of Paris. In the dense obscurity the two antagonists groped for each other, alternately guided and baffled by the light of the lanterns, as their holder lifted his light suddenly in the air or dexterously concealed it under the fold of his mantle. Every now and then the swords would meet with a clash, there would be a hurried exchange of thrust and blow, and then the adversaries would drift back again to grope and gleam and seek each other anew, their lanterns flashing and disappearing like accentuated glow-worms, and their blades now shining in sudden illumination like streaks of blue lightning across the blackness and now invisible even to those who held them in their hands.

Tristan had in vain endeavoured to persuade the king to leave before the preliminaries for the fantastic strife had been completed, but Louis was firm in his determination to remain.

"I would not miss this for the world, man," he had insisted. All his childlike delight in the adventurous was being sated to the full this evening, and there was no happier man at that moment in the kingdom than the man who by strange fortune was its king.

The fight persisted for some minutes that seemed like hours to more than one of the anxious spectators. Now the room would be steeped in the deepest silence, and now, as the revealed lantern glowed and the naked weapons met, some woman's scream or some man's suppressed oath would fill the place with a sense of watching, eager humanity.

Suddenly, when the tension of watcher and watched was keenest, there came a mighty crashing at the door and a voice shouted loudly a summons to open in the king's name.

Tristan knew well enough what the summons meant. "It is the watch, sire," he whispered to the king.

Thibaut too, groping for his nimble antagonist and beginning to despair of crushing the man, heard and understood the summons. He was tired of the baffling struggle.

"Open the door!" he shouted noisily, and the cry stirred Villon to a more vehement assault. He sprang like a cat at the giant, flashed the lantern dazzlingly in his eyes, and as Thibaut, furious, made a wild lunge at him, Villon dexterously swung his lantern on to his enemy's sword point and in another second had driven his own blade into Thibaut's side.

"Not so fast, rat-catcher!" he shouted exultantly, and as Thibaut fell with a heavy crash of rattling armour on the floor, the door was dashed open and the armed

Justin Huntly McCarthy

watch poured in with blazing torches, filling the room with light and armoured men. François, after a moment's glance of triumph at the fallen giant, sprang round and glanced up at the gallery.

Katherine, standing, leaned over the balustrade and flung a knot of ribbon to her champion, who caught it as it skimmed through the air, pressed it to his lips and thrust it into the bosom of his jerkin. In another moment Katherine had disappeared and Villon found himself roughly held in the strong grasp of two soldiers, while the captain of the watch surveyed the scene with some astonishment, and the rogues were overawed by the bills of the new-comers.

"What is this tumult?" the captain demanded. Villon answered him airily, smiling over the crossed pikes that penned him.

"A fair fight, good captain, conducted according to the honourable laws of sword and lantern."

The captain of the watch turned his attention to Thibaut, who, assisted by one of the soldiers, had raised himself upon one elbow and was glaring vindictively at Villon.

"Who is this man?" he asked.

A desire for revenge got the better of the wounded man's discretion.

"I am Thibaut d'Aussigny," he gasped. "I am the Grand Constable."

A little shiver of surprise and alarm ran round the room

at the sound of that dreaded name. The captain of the watch kneeled in salutation.

"Monseigneur," he said, "how did this happen?" Thibaut's senses were running away from him with his running blood, but malignity overcrowed weakness for a moment. He pointed at Villon. "Take that fellow and hang him on the nearest lantern," and as he spoke he swooned. Promptly the captain turned towards his prisoner. "Take that fellow outside and hang him," he commanded curtly. Villon glanced wildly about for a way to escape and saw none. His friends gave a groan of sympathy, but they could do no more, for the soldiers overawed them. Huguette flung her arms about him, sobbing. The grasp of his captors tightened and Villon shivered at the clasp. Suddenly the little insignificant burgess at the table rose and advanced towards the soldier.

"Stop, sir," he said imperatively. "That young gentleman is my affair." The soldier turned angrily upon the interfering citizen.

"Who are you," he growled, "who dare to interfere with the king's justice?"

The citizen pulled his heavy cap from his head and revealed the wrinkled, eager visage that was so well known and so well feared.

"I am the king's justice," he said simply, while Tristan behind him cried "God save the king!" and the astonished soldier bent the knee in homage. Villon, staring, dumfounded, caught the humour of the situation and could not hold his tongue.

"The king! Good Lord!" he said, and punctuated his comment with a prolonged whistle.

CHAPTER V

THE VOICES OF THE STARS

Louis loved roses. All that was royal in his nature went out to the royal flower; whatever desire of beauty lay hidden in his heart found its gratification in its splendid colours, in its splendid odours. The Greeks believed that the red rose only came into being on the fair day when Venus, seeing Ascanius slumbering on a bed of white roses, pressed handsful of the blossoms to her lips, and the pale petals blushed into their crimson loveliness beneath the kisses of the goddess. Louis the Eleventh knew nothing of the legend, but the red rose was his fancy and a corner of the royal garden was dedicated to its service. In the oldest part of the palace, hard by the grey and ancient tower where the king loved to out-watch the stars and to brood over strange wisdom, overlooked by a terrace whose very steps were littered with petals, the caressed earth glowed into a very miracle of roses. Every shade of red that a rose can wear was represented in that dazzling pleasaunce, from the faint pink that surely the lips of divinity had scarcely brushed to the smiling scarlet that suggested Aphrodite's mouth, from the imperial purple of a Caesar's pomp to the crimson so deep that it was almost black, black as the congealed blood on the torn thigh of Adonis. Here, when the stars eluded or deceived him, King Louis would come, creeping down

Justin Huntly McCarthy

the winding stairs of his tower, with the names of saints upon his thin lips, to breathe the sunlit or moonlit fragrance of his roses, to seek a little rest for his restless mind, a little quiet for his unquiet heart.

On the morning after his visit to the Fircone Tavern King Louis sat in his rose garden and snuffed the scented air with pleasure, while his keen eyes shifted from a scroll of parchment on his knee to the face of one who stood beside him, and spoke in a low voice, pointing as he spoke to marks and figures on the outspread parchment. The king's companion was an old man in a furred gown, whose countenance was seamed with years and study, and whose eyes seemed always to be gazing at objects that others could not see. In his right hand he held a large sphere of crystal, and whenever the king lapsed into silent study of his scroll the sage would lift the shining globe and gaze into its glassy depths with an air of exaggerated wisdom.

From one of these moments of abstraction the king suddenly looked up, and immediately the astrologer's glance swung from the sphere to the face of Louis.

"You know the aspect of the planetary bodies," said the king, "and you know of the strange dream that I have dreamed three nights running."

The sage inclined his head gravely. The king had told him of the dream in all its particulars at least a dozen times that morning. It seemed to be mixed up with the sunlight and the scent of the roses; to be a portion of the chorus of the birds. But he listened to the narrative with the same air of surprised attention that he had offered to its first recital.

"I dreamed that I was a swine rooting in the streets of Paris, and that I found a pearl of great price in the gutter. I set it in my crown and it filled all Paris with its light. But it seemed to grow so heavy for my forehead that I cast it from me and would have trodden it into the earth, but that a star fell from heaven and stayed me, and I awoke trembling."

The king's nasal voice droned through the familiar repetition; then he suddenly turned his head with a kind of bird-like alacrity upon the astrologer and asked sharply: "Well, what do you make of it?"

The astrologer shook his head. "The stars are bright," he said slowly, "but their brightness is bewildering to mortal eyes and it is hard to read between the lines of their effulgence. Dreams are dim, and it is difficult for mortal minds to interpret their obscurity."

The king frowned. "I know well enough," he said, "that stars are bright and that dreams are dim, but your wisdom is clothed and housed and nourished for deeper knowledge than this. Interpret my dream for France as Joseph interpreted the vision of the Egyptian."

With an unmoved face the astrologer scanned the crystal. "Thus I seem to read the riddle of your dream, sire," he answered. "There is one in the depths who, if exalted to the heights, might do you great service and who yet might irk you so greatly that you would seek to cast him back again into the depths from which he rose. The stars seem to speak of such a coming, and, as it seems to me, this stranger should have potent influence for good for a period of seven days from this day. I have sought and sought in vain to see something

Justin Huntly McCarthy

of this man in the crystal. I only see confusedly great crowds of people, pageants and masques, and movings of many soldiers, battle and bloodshed, and great victory for France - and then a star falls from heaven and all the vision vanishes."

The king was silent for a moment; then with an imperative gesture he dismissed the astrologer, who entered the tower and climbed the winding stairs to the room where he pursued his occult studies. The king walked restlessly up and down, indifferent to the roses, thinking only of the stars.

"If François Villon were the king of France," he muttered. "How that mad ballad maker glowed last night. Fools are proverbially fortunate, and a mad man may save Paris for me as a mad maid saved France for my sire."

A heavy tread behind him stirred him from his meditations. Turning, he beheld the companion of his adventure of the previous evening.

"Well, Tristan?" he questioned apprehensively, for Tristan had the evil smile on his face which he always wore when he had news of any disagreeable kind to impart.

"The bird has flown, sire," he said. "Thibaut d'Aussigny's wound was much slighter than we thought last night. After we carried him to his house, he made his escape thence in disguise, and has, as I believe, fled from Paris to join the Duke of Burgundy."

The king shrugged his shoulders indifferently.

"I wish the duke joy of him," he said. "He is more dangerous to my enemy when he is on my enemy's side. Where are the rascals of last night?"

"The tavern rabble are in custody of Messire Noel."

"And my rival for royalty?"

"Barber Olivier has charge of him. I would have hanged the rogue out of hand."

"Your turn will come, gossip, never doubt it. But the stars warn me that I need this rhyming ragamuffin. There is a tale of Haroun al Raschid - "

Tristan stifled a yawn and a sneer. "Another tale, sire," he said with something like piteous protest, for the king's tales did not always entertain Tristan.

Louis went on, however, indifferent to his companion's feelings:

"How he picked a drunken rascal from the streets and took him to his palace. When the rascal woke sober, the courtiers persuaded him that he was the Caliph, and the Commander of the Faithful found great sport in his behaviour. I promise myself a like diversion."

Tristan stared in surprise. This form of entertainment was new to him and did not seem to be particularly amusing.

"Are you going to let him think he is king, sire?" he asked.

A queer smile wrinkled the king's malign face.

"Not quite," he said. "When he wakes, he is to be assured that he is the Count of Montcorbier and Grand Constable of France. His antics may amuse me, his lucky star may serve me, and his winning tongue may help to avenge me on a certain froward maid, who disdained me. Send me here Olivier."

Tristan bowed gravely and turned on his heel. In his heart he was inclined to a kind of contempt for the monarch's humours. When there was a chance of hanging a man, it seemed to him a waste of time to play the fool in this fashion. The cat and mouse policy was never Tristan's way. He was ever for the dog's way with the rat.

Louis resumed his restless walk with his hands folded behind him and his head thrust forward as if he were scanning the ground for some lost object. His mind was busy revolving many thoughts. He knew very well how precarious his position was, how unpopular he was with his people, how strong were the forces that the Duke of Burgundy had arrayed against him, how little he could count upon the allegiance of the people of Paris if once the enemy were able to put a foot within the walls of the capital city. He was very ambitious, he was very confident, he was very brave, and yet he felt that ambition, confidence and courage were not enough at that crisis to give his throne support. The superstitious side of his nature turned restlessly to the unknown and his spirit dived into crystals or soared among the spinning planets, struggling for occult enlightenment. To the superstitious, trifles are the giants of destiny, and the king's escapade of the previous evening had taken a firm hold on his fancy. The picturesque blackguard who had mouthed so gallantly his desire to reign over France and save her would in any case have tickled the king's taste for the eccentric, but when the encounter with the poet came upon the heels of the king's strange dream and was followed by the vague prognostications of the star-gazer, the business loomed majestic in his eyes. He had always before his mind the memory of the radiant, saintly maiden who had come like a messenger from heaven to help his father when his father's fortunes seemed to be in the very dust, and it was in all seriousness that he permitted himself to hope and almost to believe that some such succour might be vouchsafed him from the fantastic rhymester who had so lately hectored him in tho Fircone Tavern. As the king lifted his eyes a fairer form than that of Villon's was impressed upon his consciousness and yet the sight only served to strengthen the current of the king's thoughts.

A very beautiful girl, tall, stately, imperious, was coming down one of the roseways with her arms full of the great crimson blossoms. If the king had been a scholar in the learning of the Greeks he would have compared the girl to some one of the glorious goddesses of the Hellenic Pantheon. As it was, he was merely aware in a fierce way that the girl was very beautiful, that her beauty appealed to him very keenly, and stirred in him a keen sense of resentment at his slighted homage. This girl, whom Thibaut d'Aussigny wanted to marry, this girl whom the king coveted, this girl whom the mad poet worshipped, what part would she play in the fantastic comedy which was gradually shaping itself in the distorted mind of Louis? Katherine de Vaucelles saw the king, and dropped him a stately curtsey.

"Where are you going, girl?" Louis asked.

She answered quietly, "To her majesty, sire, who bade me gather roses."

"Give me one," said the king, and then as the girl handed him one of the longest and reddest of her splendid cargo, the king lightly swaying the flower, brushed the girl's flower face with it and surveyed her mockingly.

"You are a pretty child," he said. "You might have had a king's love. Well, well, you were a fool. Does not Thibaut d'Aussigny woo you?"

"He professes to love me, sire, and I profess to hate him."

"He was sorely wounded last night in a tavern scuffle."

The girl gave a little cry of disappointment.

"Only wounded, sire?"

The king laughed heartily.

"Your solicitude is adorable. Be of cheer. He may recover. And we have clapped hands on his assassin. He shall pay the penalty."

Katherine drew a little nearer to the king. Her eyes were very eager, and there was eagerness in the tones of her voice.

"Sire, I bear this man no malice for hurting Thibaut d'Aussigny."

"You are clemency itself. It would never do to have a

woman on the throne. But to hurt a great lord is to hurt the whole body politic. He shall swing for it."

The girl frowned slightly.

"This man should not die, sire. Thibaut was a traitor, a villain - "

Louis' mirth deepened but he kept the gravity of his speech.

"Take care, sweeting, lest you wade out of your depth. But you women are fountains of compassion. If this knave's life interests you, plead for it to my lord the Grand Constable."

The girl made a gesture of despair.

"Thibaut is pitiless," she said. Her mouth hardened as she thought of the man she hated and of her own failure to thrust him from her path, but it softened again on the next words of the king.

"Thibaut is no longer in office. Try your luck with his successor."

She leaned forward beseechingly.

"His name, sire?"

Louis looked at her thoughtfully.

"He is the Count of Montcorbier," he said. "He is a stranger in our court, but he has found a lodging in my heart. He came under safe conduct from the South last night. He is recommended to me highly by our brother of Provence. I believe he will serve me well, and I am sure he will always be lenient to loveliness."

The king smiled affably as the ready lies slipped smoothly from his lips. He was amusing himself immensely with the threads of the fairy tale he was spinning.

"You shall have audience with him." The king paused. He caught sight on the steps of the dark familiar figure of the royal barber, who was approaching him deferentially. He called to him:

"Olivier, by and by, when my Lord of Montcorbier takes the air in the garden, bring this lady to him. You understand?"

He turned to Katherine again and once more tickled her chin with the swaying rose.

"Now, go, girl, or my wife and your queen will be wanting her roses."

Katherine again saluted the king and went slowly up the steps into the palace. Louis watched her as she went, watched her until she was out of sight, and then turned sharply upon his servant.

"Well, goodman barber, what of François Villon?"

"A pot of drugged wine last night sent him to sleep in a prison. This morning he woke in a palace, lapped in the linen of a royal bed. He has been washed and barbered, sumptuously dressed and rarely perfumed. He is so changed that his dearest friend would not know him again. He does not seem to know himself.

He carries himself as if he had been a courtier all his days."

The king chuckled.

"I have little doubt that when the jackass wore the lion's skin he thought himself the lion. But is he not amazed?"

"Too much amazed, sire, to betray amazement. His attendants assure him, with the gravest faces, that he is the Grand Constable of France. I believe he thinks himself in a dream, and, finding the dream delicate, accepts it."

"Remember," said Louis, "to keep to the tale. This fellow came here from Provence last night. None must know who he is save you and I and Tristan. Blow it about to all the court that he is the Count of Mont-corbier, the favourite of our brother of Provence, and now my friend and counsellor. I have a liking for you, Olivier, as you know, and Tristan and I are very good friends, but neither of your heads are safe on their shoulders if this sport of mine be spoiled by indiscretions."

Olivier bowed deeply.

"I cannot speak for Tristan, sire," he said, "but I can speak for myself. The God Harpocrates is not more symbolical of silence than I when it is my business to hold my tongue."

"It is well," said Louis. "I will answer for Tristan. Have this fellow sent to me here."

With another reverence Olivier left the king and ascended the steps into the palace. The king sniffed pensively at the rose which Katherine had given to him. The perfume seemed to sooth him and he mused, sunning himself and feeding his fancy with the entertainment which playing with the lives of others always afforded to him.

"This Jack and Jill shall dance to my whimsy like dolls upon a wire. It would be rare sport if Mistress Katherine disdained Louis to decline upon this beggar. He shall hang for mocking me. But he carried himself like a king for all his tatters and patches, and he shall taste of splendour."

Glancing up at the terrace he perceived the returning figure of Olivier le Dain, and guessed that his henchman was serving as herald to the new Grand Constable. Behind Olivier came a little cluster of pages, and behind them again the king could see a shining figure in cloth of gold.

"Here comes my mountebank," he said to himself, "as pompous as if he were born to the purple." He moved swiftly to the door of the tower and entered it, disappearing as the little procession descended the steps into the Rose Garden. There was a little grating in the door of the tower, a little grating with a sliding shutter, and through this grating the king now peered with infinite entertainment at the progress of the comedy himself had planned. Olivier had spoken truly when he said that Master Villon had been greatly changed. The barber's own handiwork had so cleansed and shaved his countenance, had so trimmed and readjusted his locks that his face now shone as different from the face of the tavern-haunter as the face of the moon shines from the face of a lantern. He was as sumptuously attired as if he were a prince of the blood royal: the noonday sun seemed to take fresh lustre from his suit of cloth of gold, the air to be enriched by his perfume, the world to be vastly the better for his furs and jewels. Though it was plain that the tricked-out poet was in a desperate dilemma he managed to bear himself with a dignity that consorted royally with his pomp. Olivier bowed low to the figure in cloth of gold.

"Will your dignity deign to linger awhile in this rose arbour?" he asked.

The gentleman in cloth of gold looked at him in wonder. In truth, the gentleman in cloth of gold was in a very bewildered frame of mind. He had seen but now a clean and smooth-shaven face in the mirror, with elegantly trimmed hair, and he tried to associate the image in the mirror with his own familiar face, unwashed, unkempt, unshaven. He eyed the splendid clothes that covered him and his memory fumbled in perplexity over the horrors of a dingy, filthy wardrobe, ragged, wine-stained and ancient. He looked at the solemn pages who stood about him with golden cups and golden flagons in their hands, and he tried to remember how he had escaped from the society of Master Robin Turgis into this gilded environment. His head ached with the endeavour and he abandoned it. Olivier repeated his question, and at last Villon found words, though his voice sounded strange and hollow on his ears, and hard to command.

"My dignity will deign to do anything you suggest, good master Blackamoor," he answered, but to his heart he whispered that it was better to humour these strange satellites whose persons he found it impossible to reconcile with any memories of the real world as he knew it. The barber bowed deferentially.

"I shall have to trouble you presently with certain small cares of state," he said.

Villon beamed on him benignly. He was wondering what his interlocutor was talking about, but he felt that it was the course of the wise man to betray no wonder. The conditions were, indeed, bewildering, but also they were not disagreeable, and it was as well to take them cheerfully.

"No trouble, excellent myrmidon," he answered. "These duties are pleasures to your true man."

Olivier bowed anew.

"His majesty will probably honour you with his company later."

Villon beamed again, and again his wonder found words which seemed to him to make the most and the best of the situation. Perhaps in this singular region of dreams he was the king's man and the king's friend. At least it could do no harm to assume such friendship when his solemn companion seemed to take it for granted.

"Always delighted to see dear Louis. He and I are very good friends. People say hard things of him, but believe me, they don't know him."

He was trying his best to piece together the disordered fragments of his memory and to explain to himself how it came to pass that he was on terms of friendship with the king. His head was dizzy and heavy and he felt like a man in a dark room who was groping to find the door handle. The voice of the barber interrupted these mental struggles.

"May we take our leave, monseigneur?"

Villon's face lighted. He felt that it would be pleasanter for him to be alone while he was attempting to regain control of his faculties, more especially as he noted that the pages had placed their golden cups and flagons on the marble table and that his instinct assured him that these precious vessels sheltered no less precious wine.

"You may, you may," he assented, and then as the barber made to depart, Villon's mood changed and he caught him by the sleeve and drew him confidentially toward him.

"Stay one moment," he murmured. "You know this plaguy memory of mine - what a forgetful fellow I am. Would you mind telling me again who I happen to be?"

No look of surprise stirred the barber's face; there came no change in his extreme complaisance.

"You are the Count of Montcorbier, monseigneur," he answered, gravely. "You have just arrived in Paris from the Court of Provence, where you stood in high favour with the king of that country, but your favour is, I believe, greater with the King of France, for he has been pleased to make you Grand Constable. It is his majesty's wish that you contrive to remember this."

Justin Huntly McCarthy

Villon laughed a laugh which he tried hard to make hearty and natural, but with indifferent success.

"Of course, it was most foolish of me to forget. I suppose, good master Long-toes, that a person in my exalted rank has a good deal of power, influence, authority, and what not?"

"With the king's favour, you are the first man in the realm."

Villon gave a gasp of gratification. The dream was growing in glory.

"Quite so. And does my exalted position carry with it any agreeable perquisite in the way of pocket money?"

"If you will dip your finger in your pouch - " Olivier suggested, pointing a thin forefinger at Villon's jewelled belt.

Villon thrust his fingers into the pocket that hung from it and brought them out again loaded with great golden coins, bright and clear from the mint, that gleamed joyously in the sunlight. He gave a little cry of delight as he let them run in a shining stream from hollowed hand to hollowed hand, and contemplated their jingle and glitter with the delight of a new Midas. But the first thought that welled up in his heart to welcome this strange wealth was bravely unselfish.

"Gold counters, on my honour. Dear drops from the divine stream of Pactolus. Good sir, will you straightway despatch some one you can trust with a handful of these broad pieces to the Church of the Celestins and inquire of the beadle there for the dwelling of Mother

Villon, a poor old woman, sorely plagued with a scapegrace son? Let him seek her out - she dwells in the seventh story and therefore the nearer to the Heaven she deserves - and give her these coins that she may buy herself food, clothes and firing."

He was too confused to reason clearly with his situation, but he felt sure that whoever he was and wherever he was in this amazing dream of his, the poor old woman whom he loved so well must needs be in it and might benefit by this gift of fairy gold.

Olivier bowed deferentially.

"It shall be done," he said, transferring the great gold discs to his own pocket. Then pointing to a small golden bell which one of the pages had placed upon the table, he added, "If there be anything your dignity should desire, he has only to strike upon this bell."

"You are very good," Villon responded solemnly, and on the phrase Olivier and the pages withdrew into the palace with every sign of the most profound respect. The king at his peep-hole was pleased to observe that his commands were being obeyed most strictly and that no hint of any secret mirth, no obvious consciousness of a hidden joke marred for one moment the monumental gravity of the parts which Olivier and the pages had to play.

As soon as Villon found himself alone he looked cautiously around him, comprehending in his astonished glance the grey walls of the palace, the moss-grown terrace, the petal-strewn steps, the old, stern tower with its ominous sun dial, and the wealth of wonderful roses all about him, making the air a very paradise of exquisite colours and exquisite odours. He shut his eyes for a few seconds and then opened them sharply as if expecting to find that the scene had vanished shadow-like into thin impalpable air, but castle and terrace, tower and roses remained as they had been, very plain to the poet's astonished senses. Tiptoeing cautiously across the grass, he reached a marble seat which stood beneath a bower of roses and seemed to be protected by a great terminal statue of the god Pan, which had been given as a present to Louis by an Eastern prince who had carried it from Athens. Pressing his hand to his forehead, Villon tried to recall the events of the evening before, which for some fantastic reason seemed to lie long centuries behind him. He could remember dimly an evil looking cell with straw upon the floor and chains upon the walls; he could recall the sullen faces of unfriendly gaolers. One of these gaolers he remembered had thrust a mug of wine into his hand and bade him drink surlily, and he had drunk greedily, as was his way when free drink was offered to him, and drinking, drank oblivion sudden and complete.

But why he had gone to a dungeon? His senses ached as he asked himself this, and faint pictures began to piece themselves together out of the episodes of the dead night. He saw again the squalid walls of the Fircone Tavern and his mind jumped back to his recitation of the ballad and his fierce sense of indignation at the humiliation of Paris, girdled by a wall of hostile Burgundians and governed by an impotent king. Then came the vision of an angel's visit and a prayer that had more of devil than angel in it, and then came a quarrel, and a fight in darkness shattered by the flaming torches of the watch and Thibaut's huge body lying on the ground a huddled heap of shining armour. He remembered the ribbon that had been flung to him from the gallery and thrust his hand into the bosom of his vest of cloth of gold and found the token there, its glossiness of white and gold soiled by its touch of the floor. Then came his capture, his contumelious march through the gloomy streets, his taste of an unknown prison, his taste of poppied wine, and then sleep.

His next consciousness was that he was lying on a soft bed instead of on a truss of straw, and that the darkness about him was not the darkness of the cell. Suddenly someone drew a curtain and in a second the place where he lay filled with a soft light and showed that to Villon which astonished him as much as if the gates of Paradise had parted before him and shown him the shining lines of the hosts of Heaven. He remembered that he was lying in a stately bed, nestled in snowy linen beneath a coverlet of crimson silk. He remembered that the bed stood in a gorgeous room, heavy with magnificent tapestry and roofed with a carved and painted ceiling that glittered with gilt and stars. Curtains of purple velvet admitted the daylight through windows on which rich armorial bearings glowed in coloured glass. Soft and delicate odours impregnated the atmosphere and tender strains of delicate music stole wooingly on the senses from the strings of a distant lute.

Then there carne, so kindly memory assured him, an obsequious man in black, with no less obsequious attendants, and singular ceremonies of bathing, perfuming and hair dressing and a putting on of sweet linen and furred raiment and jewels, and all the ceremonials for the transfiguration of a ragged robin into the likeness of a mighty lord. On the top of all this

Justin Huntly McCarthy

preparation rose the sun of a splendid banquet, served in ware of gold and silver and waited on by the same obsequious figure in black and the same respectful pages. Then followed the summons to walk into the air, the procession through quiet corridors on to the cool grey terrace and the final installment in the scented solitude of the rose garden. Villon was head-sick and heart-sick with the effort to put so much of the past together. He felt as if in some strange titanic way he had ruined a world and was suddenly called upon by Providence to piece the fragments together and make all whole again. He tapped his forehead wonderingly.

"Last night I was a red-handed outlaw, sleeping on the straw of a dungeon. To-day I wake in a royal bed and my varlets call me monseigneur. There are but three ways of explaining this singular situation. Either I am drunk or I am mad or I am dreaming. If I am drunk, I shall never distinguish Bordeaux Wine from Burgundy - a melancholy dilemma. Let's test it."

The marble table stood but a little way from him. The golden vessels that stood upon it had served him at that morning meal which was still an immediate excellent memory, and he remembered how his attendants had told him that one held wine of Bordeaux and one wine of Burgundy. He rose and crept across the soft grass to the table and lifted one of the golden flagons gingerly, sniffed at it fearfully and poured some of its contents carefully into a golden goblet. Lifting it cautiously to his lips, he tasted it judiciously. A ripe, warm, royal flavour rewarded him.

"By Heaven!" he cried; "no nobler juice ever rippled from Burgundian vineyards."

He drained the cup and set it down to fill another from the companion vessel and to repeat the ceremony of sniffing, tasting and swallowing. Again the desire of his palate was pleased and pacified. He reflected as he sipped and swallowed.

"This quintessence of crushed violets ripened no otherwhere than in the valleys of Bordeaux. Ergo, I am not drunk. I do not think I am mad, neither, for I know in my heart that I am poor François Villon, penniless Master of Arts, and no will o' the wisp Grand Constable. Then I am dreaming, fast asleep in the chimney corner of the Fircone Tavern, having finished that flask I filched, and everything since then has been and is a dream. The coming of Katherine, a dream. My fight with Thibaut d'Aussigny, a dream. Then the king - popping up at the last moment, like a Jack-in-the-Box - a dream. These clothes, these servants, this garden - dreams, dreams, dreams. I shall wake presently and be devilish cold and devilish hungry, and devilish shabby. But in the meantime, these dream liquors make good drinking."

He was about to fill himself another cup when a shadow fell at his feet, the shadow of Olivier le Dain standing before him with his air of emphasized respect, which was beginning to pall upon the transfigured poet.

"Your dignity will forgive me, but it is the king's wish you should pass judgment on certain prisoners."

Villon stared at him.

"I? And here?"

"Such is the king's pleasure."

"What prisoners?"

"Certain rogues and vagabonds, mankind and womankind, taken brawling in the Fircone Tavern last night."

Villon stroked his chin thoughtfully. An idea seemed to take command of his confused mind. Here was a chance to learn something of the reality that lay at the core of all this mystery of roses and wine and fine raiment. He leaned forward curiously and almost whispered to the attendant barber,

"Tell me, is Master François Villon, Master of Arts, rhymer at his best, vagabond at his worst, ne'er-do-well at all seasons, and scapegrace in all moods, among them?"

Olivier smiled complacently as those in office are accustomed to smile at the humours of great men.

"Your dignity is pleased to jest. Shall I send you the prisoners?" Villon caught at the offer sharply.

"Can I do with them as I wish?"

"Absolutely as you wish. Such is the king's will."

Villon leaned back in resigned surrender to an astonishing situation. He had dreamed strange dreams in his days and nights, but never a dream like this dream.

"Set a thief to try a thief," he philosophized, "Well,

bring them in."

Olivier bowed and disappeared silently along the rose alley by which he had come. When he was alone again Villon slapped his forehead resoundingly, as if he hoped to scare his senses back into sanity by violent assault.

"Oh, my poor head," he moaned. "Am I awake? Am I asleep? What an embroglio!"

A sense of dislike to his respectful attendant surged up through his perplexity. "That damned fellow in black is confoundedly obsequious," he muttered. "I wonder if I could order him to be hanged; he has a hanging face."

Even as this kind reflection came into his head, his meditations were disturbed by the tramp of many feet and the rattle and clank of weapons, and a small company of soldiers came wheeling round into the rose garden from the side of the palace, guarding a number of men and women, in whom Villon instantly recognized his familiar friends of the Fircone Tavern. At the head of the soldiers marched a dapper gentle-man, courtier-soldier or soldier-courtier, a thing of silk and steel, half dandy, half man-at-arms, exquisitely attired and flagrantly aware of his own attractions. He, too, was familiar to the poet, for he was no other than the pink and white gentleman whom he had seen acting as escort to Katherine on the day when he first beheld her, and whose name, as he had learned on the previous evening from Katherine's own lips, was Noel le Jolys.

"The puppet who dangles after my lady," he grumbled to himself. "He jars the dream."

Villon felt profoundly sorry for his imprisoned playfellows, and profoundly hostile to the pink and white gentleman. His friends looked so wretched, so woebegone, so bedraggled, while their captor looked so point-device and self-satisfied that Villon felt a fierce indignation burn within him over the injustices of the world.

"How hang-dog my poor devils look and how dirty," he thought to himself, as the soldiers ranged their prisoners in a line before him at the base of the terrace, and their prinked and fragrant captain came trippingly forward and saluted Villon, presenting to him at the same time a piece of paper, covered with writing.

"My lord," he said, dapperly, "here are the names of these night birds."

Villon took the paper and looked straightly into the young man's eyes.

"Have we ever met before?" he asked.

Noel le Jolys made a deprecatory gesture.

"Alas! no," he said. "Your lordship has swept into court like an unheralded comet. You shall tell us tales of Provence to please our ladies."

Still gravely looking at him, Villon questioned him again.

"Messire Noel, if you and I had a mind to pluck the same rose from this garden, which of us would win?"

The affable fribble's intelligence appeared to be baffled.

"I do not understand you," he protested.

Villon shrugged his shoulders. "Never mind," he said, seating himself again on the marble seat and looking at the familiar names on the piece of paper.

"Send me hither René de Montigny."

He was fairly convinced by this time that he was not wandering in the labyrinths of a dream, that he really was awake, but that for some reason which he was unable to fathom, he had been thus strangely transmuted into the semblance of splendour and authority.

"The popinjay fails to recognize me," he said to himself; "so may my bullies," and as he thought, René de Montigny was pushed forward by a couple of soldiers and stood sullenly defiant before him.

Villon leaned forward, oddly interested in the grotesque turn of things which put him in this position with his old companion and fellow-scamp.

"You are - " he questioned.

Montigny answered angrily,

"René de Montigny, of gentle blood, fallen on ungentle days."

"Through no fault of your own, of course?"

"As your grace surmises, through no fault of my own. I

am poor, but, I thank my stars, I am honest."

This remark, which was made aloud for the benefit of all and sundry, provoked a roar of laughter from Guy Tabarie which was promptly converted into a groan as an indignant soldier smote him into silence by a lusty blow on the back. Villon caught him up on the assertion.

"Since when, sir? Since last night?"

"I do not understand your grace."

"When Jason was a farmer in Colchis he sowed dragons' teeth and reaped soldiers. What do you grow in your garden, Sire de Montigny?"

Montigny gave a little start of surprise but his answer came prompt.

"Cabbages."

Villon shook his head. "Arrows, Master René, Burgundian arrows, most condemnable vegetables. Have a care! 'Tis a pestilent crop and may poison the gardener. Stand aside."

René de Montigny stared at his interlocutor in a paroxysm of amazement. Here was his dearest secret loose on the lips of his questioner. It was the first time that he had ventured boldly to gaze into the face of authority and Villon returned his gaze defiantly. But there was no recognition in Montigny's eyes. He could see nothing in common between the splendid gentle-man who now addressed him and the ragged rhymester who shared so many squalid adventures with him, and in an instant he averted his head respectfully.

"If your grace will deign," he pleaded, stretching out his hands in entreaty, but Villon was inexorable.

"Stand aside," he repeated, and Montigny protesting was dragged back to his place with his fellows while Villon read the name of the next rogue on the list, which happened to be that of Guy Tabarie.

By this time Villon's spirit had entered into a very complete appreciation of the humours of the situation. Having realized that his identity was safe even from the keen eyes of René de Montigny, he felt assured that he might defy the indifferent scrutiny of his less alert companions. And though he made use of the long pendant fold of his cap to conceal in some measure his countenance, he was now so confident of his safety that he was prepared to greet each prisoner with composure.

Guy Tabarie cut a piteous figure as he tottered across the grass, rudely propelled by the violence of the soldier who escorted him tweaking him by the ear, and fell, a quaking mountain of flesh, at the feet of the man whom he believed to be the Grand Constable of France. With piteous gesticulations and trembling fingers, the red, gross man knelt and attempted to plead for mercy. Villon eyed him sternly though he found it hard to restrain his laughter.

"You come with clean hands?" he asked, and Guy, answered, babbling, his words tumbling from him, incoherent and confused, holding out his huge paws like a schoolboy reproved for want of soap and water:

"As decent a lad, my lord, as ever kept body and soul together by walking on the straight and narrow path that leads to - "

He had stuttered thus far when Villon interrupted him.

"The gallows, Master Tabarie."

Guy's bulk quivered in piteous negation.

"No, no; I have the fear of God in me as strong as any man in Paris."

Villon leaned over a little nearer to his victim and breathed a question into his ear:

"Do you know the Church of St. Maturin, Master Tabarie?"

The little pig-like eyes of Tabarie widened in surprise and he stammered a "No, my lord," that was in itself a flagrant confession of shameful knowledge. Villon wagged his head wisely.

"Master Tabarie, Master Tabarie, your memory is failing you. Why, no later than the middle of March last you broke into the church at dead of night and pilfered the gold plate from the altar. The fear of God is not very strong in you."

If Master Tabarie had been listening to the words of a wizard, he could not have been more astonished.

"Saints and angels!" he cried aloud. "This Grand Constable is the devil himself! My lord, I was led astray; my lord, I was not alone - "

Villon had had enough entertainment from his fat companion.

He made a sign, and instantly a soldier swooped upon the grovelling figure, twitched him to his feet and drew him apart, stuttering furious protestations of innocence.

Villon looked at the list in his hand, and this time he called for two names, "Colin de Cayeulx and Casin Cholet," and as he spoke, the two knaves were pushed forward towards him. Villon drew the pair a little way apart and stood between them, eyeing their roguish faces on which false affability struggled with a very real fear.

"Are you good citizens, sirs?" he asked, and Colin immediately answered him:

"I am loath to sing my own praises, but I can speak frankly for my friend here. The king has no better subject, and Paris no more peaceable burgess than Casin Cholet."

As he spoke he waved Casin Cholet a warm salutation, and Cholet responded to his praises with a friendly grin and yet more friendly words:

"If I have any poor merits, I owe them all to this good gentleman's example. I have followed his lead, halting and humble. 'Keep your eye on Colin de Cayeulx,' I have ever said to myself, 'and learn how a good man lives.'"

The two men leered at each other across Villon, hoping that their praises of each other might have due effect upon the great lord who seemed so condescending to them. Villon smiled.

"You are the Castor and Pollux of purity? Do you remember the night of last Shrove Tuesday and the girl you carried off to Fat Margot's and held to ransom?"

The effect of his words upon the two men was startling. The ugly episode loomed up in their memories and they shivered to find it known. In a second the simulated friendship of bandit for bandit vanished and the two men glared at each other with the ferocity of fighting dogs as they hurled accusation and denial at each other:

"That was Colin's adventure!"

"That was Casin's enterprise!"

"I deplored it."

"I had no hand in it."

Forgetting their respect for authority in the fury of their antagonism, they struck angrily at each other across their questioner and were for grappling in close combat when Villon made a signal and they, in their turn, were dragged back raging into the ranks of their fellow prisoners.

There was only one left now - Jehan le Loup - who stood with folded arms and lowering brows, surveying the efforts of his comrades. Villon made a sign, and the man was dragged into his presence. Villon clapped him on the shoulder.

"You seem a brisk, assured fellow for a man in duress."

The friendly demeanour of the great man cheered the prisoner and he answered bluffly:

"My good conscience sustains me."

Villon's demeanour was still amicable as he put his next question in a voice that came only to Jeban's ears.

"I am glad to hear it. How did Thevenin Pensete come to his death?"

The muscles of Jehan le Loup's face twitched for a moment, but he clinched his fingers tightly to restrain himself and answered with a surly impassability,

"How should I know, my lord?"

Villon drew him nearer and spoke lower still.

"Who better? That nasty quarrel over the cards, the high words and a snatch for the winnings, a tilted table, an extinguished taper, a stab in the dark and a groan. Exit Thevenin Pensete. Your dagger doesn't grow rusty!"

Jehan's grey face grew greyer and uglier, but he kept his countenance.

"Monseigneur," he answered, "I loved him like a brother."

"As Cain loved Abel," Villon said. He made a sign, and Jehan le Loup was taken back to his fellows.

So far Villon had been sufficiently diverted. He had played upon the terrors of his friends, he had bewildered them to the top of his desire. He now foresaw the possibility of sport more delicate as his glance fell upon the group of girls who clustered together like frightened birds at the foot of the statue of Pan. He made a sign to Messire Noel, and the gilded exquisite drew near.

"Bring me hither those four gentlewomen," he commanded.

The fop's face lengthened with amazed disapprobation.

"Gentlewomen, messire? Those four doxies?"

Villon reproved him.

"They are women, good captain, and you and I are gentlemen, or should be, and must use them gently."

Messire Noel frowned and his hand made a gesture in the direction of his sword-hilt; then he remembered the folly of quarrelling with so great a man and contented himself with shrugging his shoulders as he questioned,

"And the demirep in the doublet and hose?"

"Let her stay for the present," Villon answered, and in obedience to a sign from Noel the four girls came timidly forward with downcast eyes, while Huguette remained apart, leaning composedly against the image of Pan and surveying the scene with a good-humoured indifference.

When the girls were close to him, Villon spoke:

"Well, young ladies, what is this trade of yours that has brought you into trouble?"

Jehanneton dropped a curtsey.

"I make the caps that line helmets."

Isabeau followed quickly,

"I am a lace weaver. Enne, an honest trade."

Blanche came next,

"I am a slipper maker."

Denise ended the catalogue.

"And I a glover."

Mischief danced in Villon's eyes.

"No worse and no better. A word in your ear." He whispered something into each girl's ear in turn, and as he did so, each girl started, drew back, looked confused, laughed and blushed.

It is ever to be deplored that the worthy Dom Gregory, whose ecclesiastical history of Poitou is the source of so much curious information concerning Villon, should have omitted, from a mistaken sense of delicacy, to chronicle precisely what it was that the poet whispered in the ears of each of the girls. All he condescends to record in his crabbed, canine Latin, is that Villon showed such intimate acquaintance with certain physical peculiarities or whimsical adventures private to each damsel that she believed the speaker's

Justin Huntly McCarthy

knowledge to be little less than supernatural. Literature of the skittish sort must deplore the monastic reticence, but history can do no more than accept it and leave imagination to fill in the blank as best it pleases.

All history is certain of is that the girls gathered together, chatting like sparrows, each speaking rapidly:

"The gentleman is a wizard. Why, he told me - "

"Enne, a miracle; he reminded me - "

"Why, he knows - "

"What do you think he said?"

Each girl was whispering to the other what Villon had told her, when Villon interrupted them.

"Young women, young women, the world is a devil of a place for those who are poor. I could preach you a powerful sermon on your follies and frailties, but, somehow, the words stick in my gullet. Here is a gold coin apiece for you. Go and gather yourself roses, my roses, to take back to what, Heaven pity you! you call your homes."

Jehanneton gave a little gasp of surprise.

"Are we free?"

Villon answered her sadly,

"Free? Poor children! Such as you are never free. Go and pray Heaven to make men better, for the sake of your daughter's daughters."

His extended hands were full of gold pieces, but they were soon emptied by the eager girls who pounced upon them. Then they left him with many curtsies and salutations and drifted away delightedly into the mazes of the rose garden.

Villon turned to look at the men prisoners, who were anxiously scanning his actions.

"As for these gentlemen," he said to Noel, "let them go where they will, but first give them food and drink and a pocketful of money."

The effect of his words was almost as paralyzing upon the rogues as it was upon Messire Noel. It pleased the one as much as it displeased the other.

Noel looked the contempt he did not venture to express. The men rushed forward, choking with gratitude.

"God save you, sir."

"Your Excellency is of a most excellent excellence."

"Long live the Grand Constable!"

"A most rare Constable."

Villon waved them away.

"Go your ways," he said, "and if you can, mend them."

Shouting and dancing for joy, the men took advantage of his permission and disappeared in their turn among the alleys of the rose garden, seeking and finding the wandering women and vanishing with them in due course into the labyrinths of Paris.

Villon turned to Noel.

"You may dismiss your soldiers," he said. "Attend me within call," and as Noel obeyed him, he advanced to where Huguette was standing, with a smile of scornful indifference still on her fair face.

Villon asked himself as he went:

"Why, in God's name, does the world appear so 'different to-day? Is it the thing they call the better self, or merely this purple and fine linen?"

What he said when he came to the girl was,

"Fair mistress, you have a comely face and you make it very plain that you have a comely figure. Why do you go thus?"

The girl shrugged her green shoulders and shifted the balance of her body from one green leg to the other, as she answered impudently,

"For ease and freedom, to please myself, and to show my fine shape to please others."

Last night this girl had been his own familiar friend; to-day she lay leagues away from his fairy greatness. There was pity in his next speech.

"Are you a happy woman, mistress?"

"Happy enough," she answered as she snapped her

fingers defiantly, "when fools like you don't clap me into prison for living my life in my own way."

"I may be a fool, but I did not clap you into prison. Heaven forbid!"

A curious look came into the girl's eyes, and she drew a little nearer to him. Her voice was a caress; the tenor of her hands was a caress; every supple curve of her alluring body caressed. She seemed to coax him, cat-like, as she whispered:

"Your voice sounds familiar, Monseigneur. Had I ever the honour to serve you?"

Villon drew away from her. He felt suddenly body-sick and soul-sick; sorry for the woman, sorry for himself.

"Who knows?" he answered. The girl laughed and turned aside.

"Who cares? What are you going to do with me?"

"Set you free, my delicate bird of prey. Those wild wings were never meant for clipping and caging. Is there anything I can do to please you?"

On the instant her enticement shifted; all her being was a tremulous entreaty.

"What has come to Master François Villon?"

"Why do you ask?"

"He was with us when we were snared last night. But he did not share our prison and he is not with us now.

Does he live?"

Villon hesitated for a moment before speaking.

"He lives. He is banished from Paris, but he lives."

Huguette clasped her hands in gratitude.

"The sweet saints be thanked!" she said; and there was that in her voice which made the simple words sound very sincere to Villon's ears.

"What do you care for the fate of this fellow?"

"As I am a fool, I believe I love him."

"Heaven's mercy! Why?"

"I cannot tell you, Messire. A look in his eyes, a trick of his voice - the something - the nothing that makes a woman's heart run like wax in the fire. He never made woman happy yet, and I'll swear no woman ever made him happy. If you gave him the moon, he would want the stars for a garnish. He believes nothing; he laughs at everything; he is a false monkey - and yet, I wish I had borne such a child."

There was a sudden pain at Villon's heart, as if the girl's fingers had seized it and squeezed it, but he replied lightly:

"Let us speak no more of this rascal. He believes more and laughs less than he did. He is so glad to be alive that his forehead scrapes the sky and the stars fall at his feet in gold dust. Paris is well rid of such a jackanapes."

"You are a merry gentleman."

"I would be more gentle than merry with you. Will you wear this ring for my sake? Fancy that it comes from Master François Villon, who will always think kindly of your wild eyes."

"Let me see your face," she requested, but Villon denied her. He signed to Noel le Jolys, where he stood apart, and the young soldier came hurriedly to him.

"Captain," he said, "give this lady honourable conduct."

He moved away and left the pair together - the mannish woman and the womanish man, looking at each other, the man in admiration and the woman in veiled disdain.

"You are a comely girl," Noel affirmed roundly.

Huguette laughed.

"This is news from no-man's land."

Noel spoke lower.

"Where do you lodge?"

Huguette was a woman of business in an instant. She flashed in Noel's face the ring the Grand Constable had given her as she answered:

"At the sign of the Golden Scull, hard by the Fircone. Will you visit me?"

Noel clapped his hands together.

"As I am a man, I will."

A good understanding being thus established, the pair drifted away together and were soon lost to sight. Villon looking after them mused:

"Heaven forgive me, I am becoming a most pitiful loud preacher. Every rogue there deserves the gallows, but so do I, no less, and I have not swallowed enough of this court air to make me a hypocrite. Well, all this justice is thirsty work, and, mad or sane, sleeping or waking, let me drink while I can."

He returned to the golden flagons, poured out a full cup of Burgundy, watched it glow in the sunlight, and lifted it to his lips.

"To the loveliest lady this side of heaven!" he said for a toast, but ere he touched his lips to the cup, he lowered it again.

Olivier le Dain had come on to the terrace, and with Olivier there came a lady.

"By heaven," Villon cried, "my eyes dazzle, for I believe I see her!"

CHAPTER VI

GARDEN LOVE

On the terrace the fair girl leaned and looked over at the garden and its golden occupant. To the eyes of Villon her beauty had never seemed rarer, and the wild passion which had prompted him to spin his very soul into song burnt with a new, delicious strength of hope. He stared at her as a worshipper might stare at some sudden vision of a long dreamed of goddess, and as he stared, Olivier descended the steps, soft-footed, and came and stood before him.

"My lord, there is a lady there who desires to speak with you."

Villon turned his gaze unwillingly from the gracious apparition above him to the sombre servitor.

"I desire to speak with her," he said earnestly, and again his eyes travelled in the direction of the lady.

Olivier came close to him and touched him respectfully on the wrist.

"Remember, my lord," he said, very softly, "that you are François of Corbeuil, Lord of Montcorbier, Grand Constable of France, newly come to Paris from the

Court of His Majesty of Provence. Remember this as if it were written in letters of gold upon tables of iron. Forget all else. The king commands it."

The words sounded dully enough on Villon's brain, absorbed as he was in the contemplation of his queen, but at least they served to convince him of what he had already begun to assure himself, that for some purpose or other King Louis wished him well and granted him golden chances.

François of Corbeuil, Count of Montcorbier, stood in a very different relation to the Lady Katherine from that of the lowly poet and gaolbird who had rhymed and sighed and battled in the Fircone Tavern last night.

"The king shall be obeyed," he said gravely, and Olivier, turning, made a sign to Katherine, who descended the steps slowly. As she reached the last step, Olivier saluted Villon and the lady profoundly and, mounting the steps, vanished within the palace.

The man and the woman were left alone in the rose garden. Villon felt a sudden strange sensation at his heart, exquisite pain and exquisite pleasure, and he clasped his hands together.

"I am awake," he assured himself; "no dream could be as fair as she."

Even at the thought, Katherine flung herself swiftly at his feet, divinely gracious in her surrender of dignity as she kneeled to him with uplifted imploring hands and eyes.

"My lord," she cried, "will you listen to a distressed lady?"

Villon stooped and caught her white fingers and drew her to her feet.

"Not while the lady kneels," he said gently, and he looked with a strange apprehension into the frank, bright eyes of Katherine. Would she know him for what he was, he wondered. He read no recognition in her sweet eyes. Katherine returned his gaze, unflinchingly regarding him as a great lady might regard some stranger her equal of whom she could ask a favour.

"She does not know me," Villon's delight cried in his heart, and at the thought his spirit fluttered with fierce exaltation. The Lord of Moncorbier, who was Grand Constable of France, might say many things that were denied to the lips of François Villon.

Katherine pleaded warmly:

"There is a man in prison at this hour for whom I would implore your clemency. His name is François Villon. Last night he wounded Thibaut d'Aussigny - "

Villon smiled a contented smile.

"Thereby making room for me," he suggested.

Katherine went on unheeding:

"The penalty is death. But Thibaut was a traitor sold to Burgundy."

"Did this Villon fight him for his treason?"

"No. He fought for the sake of a woman. He risked his life with a light heart because a woman asked him."

"How do you know all this?"

"Because I was the woman. This man had seen me, thought he loved me, sent me verses - "

"How insolent!"

"It was insolence - and yet they were beautiful verses. I was in mortal fear of Thibaut d'Aussigny. I went to this Villon and begged him to kill my enemy. He backed his love tale with his sword - and he lies in the shadow of death. It is not just that he should suffer for my sin."

Villon turned suddenly upon the beautiful suppliant. A thought had come into his brain so whimsical and so fantastic that it made him as dizzy for an instant as if the smooth grass beneath him had yawned into a sheer and evil precipice.

"Do you by any chance love this Villon?"

A little wave of disdain rippled over the girl's calm face.

"Great ladies do not love tavern bravos. But I pity him, and I do not want him to die, though, indeed, life cannot be very dear to him if he would fling it away to please a woman."

She had held a rose in her hand, and as she spoke she flung it from her in dainty symbolism of the life which the poor tavern poet had risked so bravely for her sake. A mad resolve came into Villon's mind. If he was, indeed, all that this woman thought him to be, all that those with whom he had spoken had assured him he was, now was his chance to play the lover to his heart's desire. If the Grand Constable had the power to pardon, surely the Grand Constable had also the right to woo. She had drawn a little way from him and he followed her up, standing so close to her that with a little movement he might have kissed her on the cheek.

"Even when you are the woman? If I had stood in this rascal's shoes, I would have done as he did for your sake."

The girl gave a joyous cry.

"If you think this, you should grant the poor knave his freedom."

Villon flung his hands apart with a magnificent gesture of liberation.

"That broker of ballads shall go free. Your prayer unshackles him and we will do no more than banish him from Paris. Forget that such a slave ever came near you."

The lady dropped him a magnificent curtsey, and her cheeks glowed with gratitude.

"I shall remember your clemency."

She made as if she would leave his presence, but his boldness waxed within him as a fire waxes with new wood, and he caught her lightly by the wrist.

"By Saint Venus, I envy this fellow that he should have won your thoughts. For I am in his case and I, too, would die to serve you!"

Surprise flamed in the girl's eyes, surprise and amusement mingled.

"My lord, you do not know me," she laughed, and her laughter was as fresh and merry as a milkmaid's in the meadows.

"Did he know you? Yet when he saw you he loved you and made bold to tell you so."

Her forehead wrinkled prettily in a little protesting frown.

"His words were of no more account than the wind in the eaves. But you and I are peers and the words we change have meanings."

Villon caught his breath. The Lord of Montcorbier was, indeed, wardered by very different stars from the fellow of the Fircone. He saluted her banteringly.

"Though I be newly come to Paris I have heard much of the beauty and more of the pride of the Lady Katherine de Vaucelles."

A little fire burned in the girl's pale cheeks, and she flung her head back scornfully.

"I am humble enough as to my beauty, but I am very proud of my pride."

Villon, leaning forward with entreating hands, pleaded

with beseeching lips.

"Would you pity me if I told you that I loved you?"

Katherine laughed, and the music of her laughter seemed to wake faint echoes among the roses as if every blossom were a magic bell with a fairy hand at the clapper.

"Heaven's mercy," she said. "How fast your fancy gallops. I care little to be flattered and less to be wooed, and I swear that I should be very hard to win."

She turned to mount the steps as she spoke, as if she had said all that she wanted to say, but Villon delayed her with imploring protest.

"I have more right to try than your taproom bandit. I see what he saw; I love what he loved."

Again the girl's laughter brightened the summer air.

"You are very inflammable."

Villon caught at her words.

"My fire burns to the ashes. You can no more stay me from loving you than you can stay the flowers from loving the soft air, or true men from loving honour, or heroes from loving glory. I would rake the moon from heaven for you."

The girl swayed her head daintily, as a queen rose might in a realm of roses. There was something like pity in her eyes, but laughter lingered on her lips.

"That promise has grown rusty since Adam first made it to Eve." She eyed him in silence for a second time, deriding his sighs with a smile: then "There is a rhyme in my mind," she cried, "about moons and lovers," and she began to declaim, half muse, half minx, some lines that had pleased her, to tease the importunate stranger.

> "Life is unstable,
>   Love may uphold;
> Fear goes in sable,
>   Courage in gold.
> Mystery covers
>   Midnight and noon,
> Heroes and lovers
>   Cry for the moon."

As the first words of the verse fell from her lips, Villon's heart leaped and his eyes brightened for he knew the sound. They were part of the rhymes himself had sent her on that very parchment which had cost him first a dinner and then a drubbing. He had fancied the words and the rhymes when he wrote them, but now they seemed to sound on his ears with the married music of all the falling waters and all the blowing winds of the world. It was a shining face that he turned to the girl as he jeered, denying the thought in his heart:

"What doggerel!"

The girl flashed scorn at him.

"Doggerel! It is divinity," she insisted, flinging a kiss from her finger-tips in Godspeed, as it were, to the banished ballad-maker, as she moved a little further up the steps. Villon followed her. Let come what might come, he was the maid's equal for the moment and would press his suit if he died for it.

"Tell me what I may do," he said, "to win your favour."

The girl's smiling face grew graver as she looked down on the imploring poet.

"A trifle," she said lightly, as a child might bid for a doll; and then, as Villon's eyes glowed questions, her voice rang out like the call of a clarion. "Save France!" she trumpeted.

Villon caught fire from both her moods.

"No more?" he said, and though the sound of his voice jested, the look in his eyes was earnest.

The girl responded to jest and earnest royally.

"No less. Are you not Grand Constable, chief of the king's army? There is an enemy at the gates of Paris, and none of the king's men can frighten him away." She pointed out where, in the distance, beyond the walls of Paris, the pitched tents of the enemy fluttered their hostile flags. Her bosom heaved with great desire. "Oh, that a man would come to court! For the man who shall trail the banners of Burgundy in the dust for the king of France to walk on, I may perhaps have favours."

Villon looked at her as men must have looked at Joan of Arc when she bade them rise up and strike for France.

"You are hard to please," he said, but his heart was full of joy at the thought of trying to please her. If he could do this thing!

The girl answered his words and not his thoughts.

"My hero must have every virtue for his wreath, every courage for his coronet. Farewell."

By this time she had reached the terrace and she made to enter the palace. Villon called to her longingly:

"Stay! I have a thousand things to say to you."

The girl smiled denial.

"I have but one," she said, "and I have said it long since. Farewell."

Villon made a dash for audacity.

"I will follow you," he said, and he moved to do so, but the girl's lifted finger stayed him.

"You may not," she said peremptorily. "I go to the queen." And so with a swift salutation, gracious as the dip of a dancing wave, she entered the palace and left him standing there, dazed and ardent, as a man might be who had just been vouchsafed the vision of an angel. He murmured to himself her words as he slowly descended the steps to the ground,

"Oh, that a man would come to court," and on that text he wove the hopeful commentary of his thoughts.

"Why should I not deserve her? Last night I was only a

poor devil with a rusty sword and a single suit. To-day all's different. I am the king's friend, it would seem, a court potentate, a man of mark. What may I not accomplish? This finery smiles like sunlight and the world will warm its hands at me."

He was exquisitely pleased with himself, exquisitely pleased with the world that held him and Katherine. He forgot, as lovers always will forget, that there was any one else in the world save himself and his beloved, and he was so wrapped in his sweet contemplations that he did not hear the tower door gently open, did not hear the soft, creeping footsteps of the king as he came out of his hiding place and shuffled across the soft grass toward his plaything.

CHAPTER VII

THE ANSWER TO BURGUNDY

A touch on the shoulder roused Villon from his honeyed meditations, and he turned with a start to find the sable figure of the king at his side and the sinister visage smiling upon him.

"Good afternoon, Lord Constable," Louis said amiably, and as Villon dropped respectfully on his knee, he questioned:

"Does power taste well?"

"Nobly, sire. On my knees let me thank your majesty."

"Nonsense, man; I'm pleasing myself. You sang yourself into splendour. 'If François were the king of France,' eh?"

Villon rose with voice and gesture of apologetic entreaty.

"Your majesty will understand - "

Louis brushed his apologies aside blandly.

"Perfectly. My good friend, you captivated me. With

what a flashing eye, with what a radiant forehead, with what a lofty carriage you thundered your verses at me. 'There,' I said to myself, 'is a real man, a man with a mission, a man who may serve France.'"

"Sire, that has been my hunger's dream of plenty."

Louis clasped his thin arms across his chest and hugged himself affectionately.

"Well, I couldn't very well make you king, you know, and I wouldn't if I could, for I have a fancy for the task myself. But I owed you a good turn and your own words prompted the payment. 'This poor devil shall taste power,' I said. 'I will make him my Grand Constable - '"

Villon's joy was so great that he was unable to hear the king out, but interrupted him with enthusiastic promises.

"Sire, I will serve you as never king was served."

Louis went on unheeding, and his quiet, monotonous words fell on the hot brain of the poet and chilled it.

"I will make him my Grand Constable for a week."

If Louis had jerked a dagger into Villon's side, he could not have more surely hurt his victim.

"A week, sire?" Villon gasped, almost unable to realize the meaning of the king's words.

Louis turned upon him and snarled at him:

Justin Huntly McCarthy

"Good Lord, did your vanity credit a permanent appointment? Come, friend, come, that would be pushing the joke too far!"

All the sunlight seemed to have gone out of the world, all the scent out of the roses. Villon could only repeat to himself: "A week!" and stare vacantly at the king. The king emphasized his offer, lingering over it lovingly.

"Even so. One wonderful week, seven delirious days." He paused for an instant as he counted. "One hundred and sixty-eight heavenly hours. It's the chance of a lifetime. The world was made in seven days. Seven days of power, seven days of splendour, seven days of love."

Villon gave a groan of despair for his golden hopes.

"And then go back to the garret and the kennel, the tavern and the brothel!"

Louis' malign smile deepened. He came closer to the poet and tapped him on the chest with his lean forefinger. He was enjoying himself immensely.

"No, no, not exactly." he hummed. "You don't taste the full force of the joke yet. In a week's time you will build me a big gibbet in the Place de Greve, and there your last task as Grand Constable will be to hang Master François Villon."

If the world had been colourless and scentless before, it was now no better than a hideous heap of ashes. If Villon had run up a heavy reckoning with the king at the Fircone Tavern, must he wipe out the score with his life-blood? Villon fell at the king's feet with extended hands and agonized, beseeching eyes.

"Sire, sire, have pity!"

The king looked down on him in disdain.

"Are you so fond of life? Are you so poor a thing that you prize your garret and your kennel, your tavern and your brothel so highly?"

Villon bowed his head.

"I was content yesterday."

The king surveyed the cowering figure with growing contempt.

"Can you be content to-day? Please yourself. There is still a door open to you. You can go back to your garret this very moment if you choose. Say the word and my servants shall strip you of your smart feathers and drub you into the street."

Villon buried his face in his hands. "Your majesty, be merciful!" he implored.

The king's scorn blazed out:

"You read Louis of France a lesson, and Louis of France returns the compliment. I took you for true gold and I am afraid that you are only base metal. You mouthed your longing for the chance to show what you could do. Here is your chance! Take it or leave it. But remember that I never change my mind. You may have your week of wonder if you wish, but if you do, by my word as a king, you shall swing for it."

Villon rose to his feet and caught at his throat as if the grip of the rope were at that very moment closing about it. He choked as he spoke.

"In God's name, sire, what have I done that you should torture me thus?"

The king snapped his answer:

"You have mocked a king and maimed a minister. You can't get off scot free."

Villon's bewildered thoughts forced themselves into words. He spoke not so much to the king as to himself, desperately trying to decide.

"Heaven help me! Life, squalid, sordid, but still life, with its tavern corners and its brute pleasures of food and drink and warm sleep, living hands to hold and living laughter to gladden me - or a week of cloth of gold, of glory, of love - and then a shameful death!"

He flung himself on the marble seat and crouched there, shuddering.

The king patted him on the back.

"Pray, friend, pray, to help your judgment!"

He had taken off his black velvet cap and ran his eye over the little row of metal saints which encircled it as if he were meditating to which particular patron he should recommend his Grand Constable to address himself. As he did so, Olivier le Dain came through the garden and moved swiftly to the king's side.

"Sire," he said, "the Burgundian herald, Toison d'Or, attends under a flag of truce with a message for your majesty."

Louis turned to his barber.

"We will receive him here, Olivier, in this green audience chamber. We need the free air when we hold speech with Burgundy."

As Olivier left the royal presence a little thing happened which meant much to four people. Katherine came on to the terrace with Noel le Jolys. She had a lute in her hand and she touched its chords lightly, seeking to make an air for words as she idled the time with her wooer. Louis saw her, though Villon did not, for he was huddled in a heap on the marble seat with his head in his hands trying to control his whirling thoughts. A new demon of mischief entered the king's heart.

"How," he thought, "if my lady Virtue, who flouted me, could be lured to love this beggar-man?" He ambled across to where Villon lay and tapped him on the shoulder. Villon turned to him a face drawn and white with agony.

"One further chance, fellow," said the king. "If the Count of Montcorbier win the heart of Lady Katherine de Vaucelles within the week, he shall escape the gallows and carry his lady love where he pleases."

"On your word of honour, sire?"

"My word is my honour, Master François. Well?"

At this very moment it pleased heaven that Katherine, sitting on the terrace and smiling at the adoration in Noel le Jolys' eyes, seemed to find the air she sought and began to sing. The tune was quaint and plaintive, tender as an ancient lullaby, the words were the words of the tortured poet, and as he heard them a new hope seemed to come into his heart.

> "Life is unstable,
>   Love may uphold;
> Fear goes in sable,
>   Courage in gold.
> Mystery covers
>   Midnight and noon,
> Heroes and lovers
>   Cry for the moon."

"Well," said the king; "you cried for the moon; I give it to you."

"And I take it at your hands!" Villon thundered. "Give me my week of wonders though I die a dog's death at the end of it. I will show France and her what lay in the heart of the poor rhymester."

Louis applauded, clapping his thin hands together gleefully.

"Spoken like a man! But remember, a bargain's a bargain. If you fail to win the lady, you must, with heaven's help, keep yourself for the gallows. No self-slaughter, no flinging away your life on some other fool's sword. I give you the moon, but I want my price for it."

Villon's blood now ran warm again in its channels, and he answered stoutly:

"Sire, I will keep my bargain. Give me my week of opportunity, and if I do not make the most of it I shall deserve the death to which you devote me."

Even as he spoke the air was stirred with a cheerful flourish of trumpets and the quiet garden was invaded by Tristan l'Hermite and a company of soldiers, escorting a tall and stately gentleman, whose gorgeous tabard proclaimed him to be Toison d'Or, the herald of the Duke of Burgundy. The news of his coming had run through the palace, and the terrace was suddenly flooded with courtiers and ladies eager to hear what the enemy's envoy had to say and what answer the king would send back to him. Louis seated himself on the marble seat anigh the image of Pan and drew Villon down beside him.

"Listen well to this man's words, my Lord Constable," he whispered, and then turning to the gleaming figure of the herald, he demanded:

"Your message, sir?"

Toison d'Or advanced a few feet nearer to the monarch and spoke in a ringing voice.

"In the name of the Duke of Burgundy and of his allies and brothers-in-arms assembled in solemn leaguer outside the walls of Paris, I hereby summon you, Louis of France, to surrender this city unconditionally and to yield yourself in confidence to my master's mercy."

The king folded his hands over his knees and inclined

Justin Huntly McCarthy

his head a little, like an enquiring bird.

"And if we refuse, Sir Herald?"

The herald answered promptly:

"The worst disasters of war, fire and sword and famine, much blood to shed and much gold to pay and for yourself no hope of pardon."

"Great words," the king sneered.

The herald replied proudly:

"The angels of great deeds."

Villon had been sitting listening as a man listens in a dream, almost unconscious of what was taking place. Among the ladies on the terrace Katherine stood conspicuous in her youth and beauty, and to her his eyes were turned in worship. The quarrels of great princes, the destinies of France were for the moment indifferent to him. He forgot his high desires of empire, his swelling belief in his real mission. He was only conscious that a great prize lay temptingly within his grasp, that he might win his heart's desire. Louis interrupted his reverie:

"The Count of Montcorbier, Constable of France, is my counsellor. His voice delivers my mind. Speak, friend, and give this messenger his answer."

He touched Villon on the arm and Villon turned to him in astonishment. "As I will, sire?"

The king caught him up impatiently.

"Yes, go on, go on. 'If Villon were the king of France.'"

Villon leaped to his feet and advanced toward the herald. A wild exultation filled his veins with fire. He felt as if he were the lord of the world, as if his hands held the scales that decided the destinies of nations. He had always dreamed of the great deeds he would do, and now great deeds were possible to him, and at least he would try to do them. He looked straight into the herald's changeless face, but his heart shrined Katherine as he spoke.

"Herald of Burgundy, in God's name and the king's, I bid you go back to your master and say this: Kings are great in the eyes of their people, but the people are great in the eyes of God, and it is the people of France who answer you in the name of this epitome. The people of Paris are not so poor of spirit that they fear the croak of the Burgundian ravens. We are well victualled, we are well armed; we lie snug and warm behind our stout walls; we laugh at your leaguer. But when we who eat are hungry, when we who drink are dry, when we who glow are frozen, when there is neither bite on the board nor sup in the pitcher nor spark upon the hearth, our answer to rebellious Burgundy will be the same. You are knocking at our doors, beware lest we open them and come forth to speak with our enemy at the gate. We give you back defiance for defiance, menace for menace, blow for blow. This is our answer - this and the drawn sword. God and St. Denis for the King of France!"

As he spoke, he drew his sword and flashed it aloft in the sunlight. There was contagion in his burning words, and every soldier present bared his blade and pointed it to heaven while Villon's cry was repeated upon a hundred lips. As Toison d'Or turned and left the presence, Katherine came swiftly down the steps and flung herself at Villon's feet.

"My Lord," she said. "With my lips the women of France thank you for your words of flame."

Louis leaned forward, smiling sardonically.

"Mistress, what does this mean?" he questioned.

The girl rose to her feet, looking into Villon's face with eyes that mirrored the admiration shining in his eyes.

"It means, sire, that a man has come to court!"

CHAPTER VIII

A WORD WITH DOM GREGORY

It is a thousand pities that the materials for building up a practical presentment of the real life-story of Master François Villon are so slight, that in the historical sense they might almost be said to be non-existent. We know, indeed, a little of Master François' early days, partly from some confessions which must at all times be interpreted with a liberal sense of humour and glossed with an infinite deal of good nature, and partly from stray records made by those who do not seem to have held the vagrant poet very warm in their hearts. But of his life in those days of which this chronicle deals, there is little to find where there is much to seek.

The silence of Commines may be explained in a thousand ways, possibly professional jealousy of one minister for another, who in so short a space of time did so much and so well, possibly ignorance of the real facts of the case, for it is fairly certain that King Louis kept his jape and its sequel very much to himself, possibly because Commines felt that his cold spirit was scarcely equal to the proper recording of so whimsical and oriental an adventure.

Good Master Clement Marot, when he took it upon himself, generations after our poet was dust and ashes, to edit our poet's writings, said much in praise of the singer but said little, no doubt because he knew little, of the poet's life.

And the great creator of Pantagruel and Gargantua, the immeasurable Alcofribias Nasier, whom the world loves or hates as Rabelais, in what he contributed to our knowledge of François Villon has only - to use a weather-worn and moss-grown phrase - made confusion yet worse confounded.

We should be at a deadlock, indeed, if it were not for Poitou and its Abbey of Bonne Aventure, whose library is luckily rich in historical manuscripts of the period, and richest of all in that priceless manuscript of Dom Gregory, which, treating in general of the ecclesiastical history of Poitou in the fifteenth century, dealt so particularly and so liberally with the life of Master François Villon, because Master François Villon in his old age was so excellent a patron of the church. We say dealt advisedly, for time has treated somewhat scurvily the fair skins of parchment upon which the good Dom Gregory recorded his thoughts and his opinions at considerable length as the rich setting of the facts, too few in number, with which he condescended to enlighten posterity. Many pieces of parchment are missing from the roll of his record, and, unhappily, the greatest gap in the story is precisely at that point where our hero found himself so suddenly and so strangely taken into favour by his king, and so suddenly and so strangely smiled upon by his mistress. We have indeed some admirable homiletics of the worthy friar's in praise of the conduct and carriage of Master François Villon at the time of his unexpected exaltation. After a gracious invocation of many saints and angels, the very elect of the company of heaven,

Dom Gregory, in a fine spirit of rectitude, proceeds to applaud the Count of Montcorbier for the high example he set to his fellow-men. Here, in effect says the worthy churchman, was a man who, having passed the flower of his life in squalor and all manner of ignobilities, still kept in a sense the whiteness of his soul and allowed the brightness of the celestial flame to burn, faintly indeed but unextinguished, on the altar of his heart. How many men, asks Dom Gregory, glowing with a pious gratification, how many men who in humility have dreamed that they might under serener stars and happier auspices do great deeds and win honourable honours, would, if put to the proof, show themselves as splendid in prosperity as they dreamed themselves in adversity? Master François Villon, he goes on to say, is the loveliest example known to him of a man, who, having always believed in himself with a great belief, did, on being put to the test, prove that his belief was founded, not on the shifting sands of vanity and vain glory, but on the solid granite of good faith and the inestimable doctrines of the church.

From all this we gather dimly, as one discerns objects in a mist, that Master François Villon, as Count of Montcorbier, proved nimself to be little less than equal to the high opinion of himself which he had confided all unwittingly into the ear of his masquerading sovereign. But the pages in which Dom Gregory sets forth at length exactly all that Master François Villon did and said and thought during the period of his astonishing probation, are unfortunately lost to the Abbey of Bonne Aventure, and, in consequence, to the world. No less than six folios consecrated by the careful pen of Dom Gregory to this memorable epoch have vanished from the priceless manuscript. The custodian of the Abbey library will tell you with tears in his eyes that these pages disappeared during the storm and stress of the French Revolution, but travellers in France are too well aware of the readiness of ecclesiastical custodians to attribute all things evil to the time of the great upheaval, to pay any serious attention to this particular allegation. However it happened, the pages are lost, and there, as far as we are concerned, is an end of them.

But in a way we are able to piece together from Dorn Gregory's later statements, and from certain traditions which still linger here and there in the highways and byways of Poitou, enough material to enable us to ascertain with something like sufficient accuracy, what it was that Master François Villon did accomplish as Count of Montcorbier in those seven days of splendour which his mocking king accorded to him. We know for certain that the king found him an admirable counsellor, cool, wary and judicious, and that during the period of his ministry, Louis followed his advice with a faith which, if it were founded indeed upon a superstitious adherence to the edicts of the stars, proved itself to be thoroughly justified by his Lord Constable's common sense, foresight and astonishing knowledge of human nature. We know, too, that he proved himself no less skilled as a soldier than as a statesman, as capable of pre-eminence in the arts of war as in the arts of peace. His knowledge of Caesar's Commentaries and his natural inclination to strategy, interpreted by an eloquent tongue fired by a ready mother wit, earned him the ear and won him the heart of the king's great captains and wrung from them at first a reluctant but finally such a delighted adherence as their sires had been compelled to surrender to the Maid of Orleans.

Yet while our poet was playing these two parts, he managed his affairs so dexterously that he seemed to the general eye to be playing but one part, and that the part of the dazzlingly magnificent courtier. If his mornings were given to consultation with the king and the king's chief soldiers, if his forenoons were devoted to the confirming of edicts and the promulgations of laws all tending to alleviate the condition and lighten the load of the people of Paris, his afternoons and evenings and shining summer nights were entirely surrendered to the glittering pleasures and pastimes of a man of ease. We hear of entertainment after entertainment, banquet and ball and masquerade, pageant and play and pastime, each one of which seemed to be the last word of wealthy ingenuity until it was eclipsed by its still more splendid successor. And it was this part of which the Count of Montcorbier chose to make the most with a very special purpose. He caused, it seems, many emissaries of his to quit Paris and find shelter within the Duke of Burgundy's lines, pretending to be deserters from the waning cause of the king, each of whom had the same tale to tell to the credulous ears of the enemy; namely, that the king's new favourite was a wastrel and a fool, who had no better pu rpose in life than the rhyming of madrigals, the tuning of lutes, the draining of flagons, and the pressing of ladies' fingers in the dance. All of which produced, we are assured, upon the mind of the Duke of Burgundy the very effect desired by Villon and led to results which luckily we are enabled to know more of, as Dom Gregory's manuscript happily resumes continuity on the seventh day of Master François' week of wonder.

We further learn - for Dom Gregory, though a churchman, seems to have a kindly spot in his heart for the ways of lovers - that during those seven days, the friendship of Villon and Katherine grew apace and that the whole court watched with interest, and Monsieur Noel le Jolys with an ever-increasing fury, the growth of a great and beautiful passion. But it seems that Master Villon, whether from fear to risk too soon or from a desire to leave the loveliest moment of his reign to the last, made no attempt directly to declare himself or directly to learn how high he stood in the Lady Katherine's heart until the very day which was the last day upon which it was possible for him to assure his own salvation.

CHAPTER IX

IF I WERE TO DIE TO-MORROW

On the seventh day of Villon's week of wonder, his glory was at its greatest. No fairer day had traced that radiant month of June and no more splendid pageantry had adorned the illustrious reign of the new Grand Constable. Mimic battles, fountains running wine, free doles of food, fantastic pageants, grotesque dances, all the gorgeous mummery that the fifteenth century delighted in was offered in profusion to please the fancy and win the hearts of the people of Paris. But the crowning triumph was the great festival which the Grand Constable gave with the king's permission in the king's own rose garden, the magnificent mascarado in the Italian manner, to which all who were associated with the court were summoned. This revelry which began at sunset was intended to overtop all possible courtly ceremonials in the splendour of its equipment, the lavishness of its display, the richness and profusion of its hospitality.

It was near to the hour of sunset when Villon sat with the king in the little room in the grey tower from which the king loved to follow the movements of the heavenly bodies. On the table by which the king and Villon were seated lay a large chart of the country in the immediate neighbourhood of Paris, and in front of

Justin Huntly McCarthy

the table stood three of the king's most trusty commanders, the Lord du Lau, the Lord Poncet de Riviere and the Lord of Nantoillet.

Villon had been explaining to the king and to his military advisers a scheme which had been growing in his mind throughout the week for the confusion of the enemy, a scheme for which the gorgeous entertainment to be given that evening was to serve as a golden mask. Villon touched a point on the map which represented a spot very familiar to him, a little dip in the swelling land, where he used to play as a child and gather wildflowers and hide himself, and imagine that he was a bandit or a great captain or a fairy prince - any one of the thousand illusions of childhood at its play.

"There, sire," he said. "If we can lure the Burgundians to that hollow, the day is ours. The sloping ground above it will mask a thousand men."

Poncet de Riviere leaned forward questioningly.

"Are you sure of the lay of the land?"

Villon answered positively:

"Sure. I played truant there when I was no higher than your sword belt."

Nantoillet spoke as a man who weighs his words:

"The scheme seems feasible, sire."

Villon glanced up from the table in humourous apology.

"You may think me a raw soldier," he said; "yet I have practised strategy all my days."

Du Lau answered him approvingly:

"My lord, you reason like a seasoned veteran."

Pleased with the praise Villon turned to the king.

"Sire, I have blown it abroad that your majesty feasts to-night. While the Duke of Burgundy believes us to be carousing, we shall make a sortie from St. Anthony's gate. Our horses' hooves will be muffled, no spur shall jingle, and no bridle clink. We will steal through the night like shadows. At the cross road some few of us will make an attack upon the enemy's left and beat a retreat. This will tempt him into our ambuscade and as I believe end in his rout. At nine, my lords. Farewell."

He raised his hand in dismissal; the three captains saluted the king and his minister and passed out of the presence. As they descended the winding stairs, du Lau said to his companions:

"I do not know your hearts, my lords, but I love this soldier of fortune."

Nantoillet answered cordially:

"God knows where he came from and God knows where he will go to, but I would ride with him to the world's end."

"My father," said Poncet de Riviere, "told me often of the Maid of Orleans and her power with bearded men.

He must be of her kindred, for he wins me against my will."

As the sound of their feet died away in the depths of the tower, Villon turned to the king.

"If the Duke of Burgundy falls into my trap," he said; "men will call me a great captain. Yet it is no more than remembering the shape of a meadow where I played in childhood. Strange that an urchin's playground should become a Golgotha of graves and glories."

The king clapped him playfully on the shoulder.

"Where did you learn wisdom?"

"In the school of hope deferred. When I was - what I was, I still believed that this dingy carcass swaddled a Roman spirit. In the pomp of my pallet I dreamed Olympian dreams. And the dreams have come true."

"You are an amazing fellow. Here in a week, you have made me more popular than I made myself since my accession. In court, in camp, in council, men are pleased to call you paragon."

"I am a man of the people and I know what the people need. A week ago the good people of Paris were disloyal enough. I repeal the tax on wine and to-day they clap their hands and cry 'God save King Louis' lustily. A week ago your soldiers were mutinous because they were ill fed, worse clothed, and never paid at all. I feed them full, clothe them warm, pay them well, and to-day your majesty has an army that would follow me to the devil if I whistled a marching tune."

"But in the meantime, your sands are running out. Is your heart failing? Is your pulse flagging?"

"Not a whit. I have been translated without discredit from the tavern to the palace, and if the worse comes to the worst, I may say with the dying Caesar, 'Applaud me.'"

The king grinned sardonically.

"Will the worse come to the worst?" he piped, "How is your suit with the Lady Katherine?"

Villon's smile lingered still on his lips as he answered:

"Sire, no wise man boasts that he knows the heart of a woman, and yet, I hope for the best."

"But if you fail," the king persisted.

Villon's smile grew more philosophical. In his heart he felt fairly confident, but spoke cautiously.

"Why, then, when the housewife moon kindles her pale fire on the hearth of heaven to-morrow, I shall be quiet enough. But either way you have given me a royal week, and I have made the most of it, lived a thousand lives, eaten my cake to the last sweet crumb and have known the meaning of kingship."

Louis laughed.

"You speak as if you had reigned for a century."

Villon's sententious mood deepened.

"A man might live a thousand years and yet be no more account at the last than as a great eater of dinners. Whereas to suck all the sweet and snuff all the perfume but of a single hour, to push all its possibilities to the edge of the chessboard, is to live greatly though it be not to live long, and an end is an end if it come on the winged heels of a week or the dull crutch of a century."

Louis leaned back and looked at his companion in astonishment.

"Pray heaven this philosophy may sound as fine when your neck is in the halter."

"Your majesty's wit and my wish run nose and nose in a leash."

Louis changed the subject as if there were more important matters in the world than the life, loves and death even of a Grand Constable.

"Messire Noel brings me a new astrologer to-night. The heavens seem in a conspiracy of confusion, the stars are all a tangle! My dream of a star falling from heaven defies divination."

Villon looked at him pityingly.

"Do you never tire of these sky doctors?" he questioned.

Louis frowned, as he always frowned at any hint of disbelief in the science of the stars.

"Don't jest, master poet," he said, "but ply your suit with proud Kate, for I swear if you fail, you shall hang to-morrow. Now leave me, for I must work while you play," and he bent over a chart and seemed to forget all else in his profound contemplation.

Villon looked at him for a moment in silence and then went out of the room and descended the steps, opened the little door, and passed into the garden. The summer sun was dying in a splendid riot of colour among the rose trees. Its last rays, falling on the face of the god Pan, illuminated his fantastic features and seemed to lend them the life of an ironic leer. The warm air was rich with the blended odours of a thousand blossoms, and from the palace, faint and far off, came the sound of joyous voices. It was almost the moment when the rose garden was to be thrown open to the royal guests.

Villon pulled a rose from a bush by his hand and gazed into its crimson heart as if he sought to read there the secret which all flowers hold but which no flower has ever yet betrayed to the longing eyes of a poet. He leaned against the statue of Pan and mused pensively.

"The petals of my reign are falling from me full of life, full of colour to the end. Shall I win this wonderful woman? Am I mad to hope it? If I lose, it is a short shrift and a long rope at the end of a dazzling dream."

He shivered as he thought and cast the rose he held away from him.

"How cold the June air seems, and these roses smell of graves." He paused a little till his hopes took heart again. "But if I win, how will it be, I wonder, to marry my heart's desire, to grow old sedately, to live again with the children on my knee, a little François here more honest than his father, a little Katherine there less comely than her mother!"

He flung out his hands as if he were dismissing the phantoms of his fancy.

"Run away, my dear dream children to your playground of shadows where you belong, for your father may be hanged to-morrow, and he fights for love and life to-night."

Villon's reflections were fluttered by a sudden blare of music, and a gaudy fellow in a pursuivant's coat made his appearance on the top of the terrace and rattled blast after blast from his brazen trumpet. In obedience to the long-looked-for signal, a many-coloured crowd of revellers gushed from the palace and flowed like a glowing wave of merry-making down the steps and into the walks and alleys of the rose garden. All the strange figures that a freakish fancy could suggest leaped and danced and shouted in a rapture of mirth-satyrs and follies, clowns and devils wheeled wildly by, waving torches, clashing cymbals, or screaming at the top of their voices, while sedater spirits, masked and muffled in mantles of sombre hue, moved through the tumultuous throng and found their abated pleasure in mystification and intrigues.

Villon had a mask in his girdle. He put it on and pushing into the press allowed himself to drift hither and thither with the eddying currents of pleasure. His fantastic imagination took fire from the strange shapes and sounds about him. The sense of being in a dream, which had never deserted him from the first moment of his awakened consciousness in the rose garden, clung closely about him on this night, and the jocund figures around him flitted by as unreal as the phantoms of a noon-tide sleep.

Suddenly his attention was arrested by the sound of a voice that seemed familiar to him. A man habited like a pilgrim from the Holy Land, in long hood and gabardine of grey, and with the pilgrim's cockleshell on his shoulder, had met another masker, habited like himself. The pair were exchanging salutations, in a speech that the speakers might well assume to be unknown to any person in the royal garden. The speech, however, jingled very familiarly on Villon's ear, for the man was talking in the amazing jargon which the worshipful company of cockleshells had devised for the better furtherance of their thievish purposes, and it appealed to Villon as intimately as a song that is learned in childhood.

The first pilgrim questioned the other,

"What do you carry in your scrip?"

And the second answered:

"I carry a cockleshell."

The first pilgrim questioned again:

"What do you carry in your hand?"

And the second responded:

"A foot of steel."

Yet again the first speaker queried:

"Will you drink the king's health?"

And the answer came decisively:

"In a flagon of Burgundy."

Whereat the two pilgrims saluted and parted and went their several ways and were swallowed up in the motley masquerade.

Villon's curiosity was piqued to the quick.

"How in heaven's name," he asked himself, "does it come to pass that people speaking the thieves' lingo of the Court of Miracles find themselves at a feast in the rose garden of King Louis?"

He set himself to try and track down one or the other of the mysterious pilgrims, but neither of them was to be found. His wanderings brought him back to the fair space at the foot of the terrace protected by the image of the god Pan. The place was deserted; the revellers had drifted elsewhere. A lute lay on the marble seat. Villon seated himself and taking up the instrument was touching it carelessly, when a light step on the grass arrested him, the sweetest voice in the world sounded in his ears, and he found himself addressed by the Lady Katherine de Vaucelles, who was attended by a number of fair court ladies.

"I am the voice of these ladies to pray for a favour."

Villon bowed low.

"My ear is all obedience," he said, "and my heart all homage."

"You are a poet, my lord," said Katherine, "and this is an eve which should please a poet. Rhyme us a rhyme which shall match this night of summer."

Villon sighed a little.

"No rhyme ever rhymed was worth a beam of summer sun or summer moon; but I have lingered in Provence where every man is a nightingale, and I caught there the fever of improvisation. What shall I rhyme about?"

Katherine laughed as she pointed to her attendant ladies.

"Your suitors are women; therefore, nothing better nor worse than love."

"The burden of the world," Villon said. "Sigh, my lute, sigh."

He let his fingers ripple over the strings, waking the faint wail of a plaintive minor. In a moment or two he began to recite, touching every now and then a chord on his lute to emphasize the words he spoke:

> "I wonder in what Isle of Bliss
>   Apollo's music fills the air;
> In what green valley Artemis
>   For young Endymion spreads the snare:
> Where Venus lingers debonair:
>   The Wind has blown them all away -
> And Pan lies piping in his lair -
>   Where are the Gods of Yesterday?
>
> "Say where the great Semiramis
>   Sleeps in a rose-red tomb; and where

The precious dust of Caesar is,
  Or Cleopatra's yellow hair:
Where Alexander Do-and-Dare;
  The Wind has blown them all away -
And Redbeard of the Iron Chair;
  Where are the Dreams of Yesterday?

"Where is the Queen of Herod's kiss,
  And Phryne in her beauty bare;
By what strange sea does Tomyris
  With Dido and Cassandra share
Divine Proserpina's despair;
  The Wind has blown them all away -
For what poor ghost does Helen care?
  Where are the Girls of Yesterday?

"Alas for lovers! Pair by pair
  The Wind has blown them all away:
The young and yare, the fond and fair:
  Where are the Snows of Yesterday?"

The little group whom he addressed lingered in a gracious silence for a short space. Singer and listeners seemed to be in an exquisite isolation of moonlight and soft odours. Katherine murmured pensively to herself:

"Where are the snows of yesterday?"

Her eyes were shining like summer stars, her parted lips made Villon think of ripe pomegranates, her mind was wandering in the Islands of the Blest with the lovers and ladies whom Villon had praised. Villon dismissed melancholy with a jest:

"Sweet ladies," he said; "my song is sung. Do not let it dishearten you, for, believe me, it will snow again next year and lie white and light on the graves of dead lovers. Yesterday is dead, and to-morrow comes never."

He drew very close to Katherine and whispered the end of his
sentence in her ear:

"Let us live and love to-day."

Katherine gave a little start as she dropped from cloudland and looked at him. He drew back and turned to the others.

"Fair ladies," he said; "shall we go to the great hall where the Italian players gambol?"

The women gathered about him, thanking him for his song, and then fluttered away like brilliant birds, up the steps to the terrace. As they did so a figure in a pilgrim's gown came from the scented gloom of one of the rose alleys, paused for a moment as if undecided as to his course, and then proceeded to cross the space of moonlit grass. He did not heed Katherine, standing in the shadow, till he almost touched her. Then he glanced at her, and with a stifled exclamation hurried past, plunged into the darkness of an opposite alley, and disappeared. Katherine gave a little cry that was almost a cry of fear, and ran swiftly to where Villon stood apart at the foot of the steps awaiting her pleasure.

"My lord!" she cried, and he, turning, swiftly responded:

"My lady!"

"This masking kindles fancies. I thought but now that the eyes of Thibaut d'Aussigny glared on me from under a pilgrim's hood."

Villon frowned.

"A villainous apparition. For the news is that he lies dead in the camp of Burgundy."

Katherine gave a little shudder.

"I always hated him; almost feared him. If he be dead, I hope he will not haunt me. Ah! I tingle to-night like a lute that is tuned too high."

"Let us think of no evil things to-night," Villon responded. "Will you watch the players?"

Katherine shook her head.

"Nay, I am more in a mood for moonlight than candlelight."

Villon looked at her in silence, a silence of seconds that seemed to both of them like the silence of hours. The hearts of both were houses of sweet hopes, and the brains of both were hives of happy thoughts.

"May I ask you a question?" Villon said, and the girl answered:

"Surely."

"Are you content with me?"

"You have done much."

"I have more to do. For seven days I have wrestled with greatness as Jacob wrestled with the angels; I have made the king popular, the Parisians loyal, the army faithful - "

"Then why do you linger here where courtiers feast and ladies dance?"

Villon's voice swelled proudly as he answered:

"I want the Duke of Burgundy to believe that the king's favourite is a zany, and the king's court an orgy, where the king's honour melts like a pearl in a pot of vinegar. But our swords are tempered in wine and sharpened to dance music, and to-night we ride."

The girl sighed. "I would that I were a man that I might ride with you."

Villon came close to her and peered into her eyes.

"I ride in your honour. Heaven has been very good to me, and I serve France serving you. Perhaps I serve both for the last time."

"For the last time?" she repeated.

"Even so, my sweet Lady Echo. Those far away lanterns warn me that I may die to-morrow. Some of us will be dreaming our last dreams by sunrise. I may be one of those heavy sleepers."

"Why, you may die if you ride on the king's business, but so may I who sit at home and eat my heart."

"For whom?"

"I will tell you that to-morrow."

Villon touched her lightly on the wrist and pointed to the grey tower on whose weather-beaten wall the quaint old dial showed plainly in the bright moonlight, with its wise Latin inscription: "Dum Spectas, Fugit Hora, Carpe Diem."

"There is no time like now time. That dial there is as wise as the wisest." And he rapidly rendered the antique maxim into a running rhyme:

> "Observe how fast time hurries past,
>   Then use each hour while in your power;
> For comes the sun but time flies on,
>   Proceeding ever, returning never."

Katherine tried to laugh.

"This was old wisdom when Noah sailed the seas," she said, and drew a little apart from him. Villon followed her.

"Well, let to-morrow tell to-morrow's story. To-night I feel like a happy child in a world of make-believe. To-night we are immortal, you and I, wandering forever in this green garden under those indifferent stars, breathing this rose-scented air, spelling the secret of the world."

"You may say what you please to-morrow," she whispered, but Villon would not have it so.

"Alas, no! To-morrow I shall be mortally sober; to-night I am divinely drunk-drunk with star wine, flower wine, song wine. The stars burn my brain; the roses pierce my flesh; the songs trouble my soul. To-night, if I dared, I would ease my heart."

The girl spoke so faintly that only a lover's ears could hear the words:

"You may say what you please to-night."

Villon caught at his heart as if to keep it in the compass of his breast.

"If I were to die to-morrow, I would tell you this to-night: I love you. These are easy words to say, yet my heart fails as I say them, for their meaning is as full and musical as the Bell of Doom. Men are such fools that they have but one name for a thousand meanings, and beggar the poor love-word to base kitchen usages and work-a-day desires. But I would keep it holy for the flame which it sometimes pleases heaven to light in one heart for the worship of another. I never knew what love was till I saw a girl's face on a May morning and wisdom stripped the rind from my naked heart. The God in me leaped into being to greet the God in your eyes. I love you. This is what I would say if I were to die to-morrow."

He was very close to her now, and his eyes were looking into her eyes. She answered him frankly:

"If you were to die to-morrow, I might tell you this much to-night. A woman may love a man because he is brave, or because he is comely, or because he is wise, or gentle - for a thousand thousand reasons. But the best of all reasons for a woman loving a man is just because she loves him, without rhyme and without reason, because heaven wills it, because earth fulfils it, because his hand is of the right size to hold her heart in its hollow."

The lovers' hands were closely clasped, the lovers' lips were very near to meeting. Only the god Pan smiled and sneered as if he knew that sometimes lovers' lips fail to meet even when the space between fervent mouth and mouth is no bigger than a rose-leaf.

"Katherine," Villon whispered, and drew her closer to him. Love, happiness, life were coming to his arms as to a shrine.

In the sudden bliss that had come upon both the lovers they paid no heed to a footstep upon the terrace, till a voice struck like a sword-stroke across their ecstasy, the voice of Noel le Jolys.

"Where are the lovers of yesterday?" Noel said mockingly as he slowly descended the steps to join them.

There was a red rage in Villon's heart, but he bridled it as he turned upon the interloper contemptuously.

"Your pink and white lady-bird," he said to Katherine, and then waving his hand at Noel with a gesture of disdain and dismissal, chanted at him:

"Lady-bird, lady-bird, fly away home."

Noel's pink face flushed a poppy red and his white hand went to his sword hilt. There was courage in the foppish substance, and he would clearly have rejoiced to try his chance in a passage-at-arms.

"My lord," he said, "I will measure word and sword with you at any season, but now I seek promised speech with this lady."

Villon laughed at his menace.

"While I have better business in hand, you shall know only the smooth of my tongue and the flat of my falchion. Compass your swelling heart lest you play the lion before a lady."

The two men eyed each other like angry dogs, eager to spring at each other's throats. Katherine dropped her restraining hand on Villon's arm.

"My lord," she whispered, "he has importuned me for audience. I will speak with you again ere you ride."

Villon turned to her.

"We ride at nine, remember," he said in a low voice; and then in a louder tone, looking at Noel, he added mockingly, "Till then I shall busy myself in writing my last will and testament, and bequeathing a thousand nothings to a thousand nobodies to puzzle posterity. You shall taste of my bounty, Messire Noel," and he began to improvise derisively:

> "To Messire Noel, named the neat
> By those who love him, I bequeath
> A helmless ship, a houseless street,
> A wordless book, a swordless sheath,
> An hourless clock, a leafless wreath,
> A bed sans sheet, a board sans meat,
> A bell sans tongue, a saw sans teeth,
> To make his nothingness complete."

Noel shrugged his shoulders and turned his back. He was very irate, but he was resolved to show nothing but indifference.

"Do you leave me nothing?" Katherine whispered, and Villon answered:

"Now and always the heart of my heart."

He turned on his heel and glided into the liquid darkness of the rose alley, alone with exquisite thoughts.

Katherine turned to Noel haughtily.

"Well?" she said.

"I have always to seek you nowadays," Noel protested.

Katherine tossed her head, and her tresses trembled like leaves in the moonlight.

"The world is not yet so old that the wooing must be done by women."

"I am out of favour," Noel complained, "since a fellow from nowhere plays the fool in high places."

Katherine's eyes showered scorn upon him.

"I do not hate you for railing at him, but it does not help me to love you."

Noel caught at the word.

"You loved me once," he asserted.

She shook her head pityingly.

"We played with great words as children play with coloured balls. It is easy to say 'I love you,' and often very sweet; yet the coloured balls roll into the corner, and the child forgets them when the moon of childhood wanes."

A wistful irritation puckered Noel's smooth countenance.

"You have outgrown me?" he questioned.

Katherine drew away from him till the moonlight that shone between them lay wide and white. She answered quietly:

"My soul was in bud a week ago. To-day it is in blossom."

Noel threw up his arms impatiently.

"God have mercy! What can this fellow do that is denied to me? Can he stride a horse, or fly a hawk better? show a brighter sword in quarrel, or tune a smoother lute in calm? Can he out-dance me, out-drink me, out-courtier me, out-soldier me? No, no, no! And must I now believe that he can out-love me?"

Katherine, weary of the controversy, began to ascend the steps to the palace. She spoke as she mounted:

"When a man comes to court, it is worth while to be a woman. You will learn that some day, Sir Noel, if you grow to be a man."

Noel retorted:

"It is no great blazon to be the favourite of a king. Gentlemen who brag little may do much. The old love may outlast the new."

Katherine frowned at his mystery.

"You speak like a scented Sphinx, but I am too idle for enigmas. Farewell!" and she vanished into the palace.

Noel looked after her fretfully:

"Why are the women all sunflowers to this scara-mouch?" he asked himself querulously. "Well, there are other women, and a wise man gathers the nearest grapes."

A flagon and cup stood on the table by the marble seat. Noel poured himself out some wine and drank it, seeking consolation. His duty called him shortly to the service of the king, but he lingered in the garden on the chance of a hoped-for meeting.

"I shall be revenged," he said to himself, "if my astrologer plays his part and tells the weak king that this Lord of Montcorbier is his evil spirit."

His thoughts were busy with the events of the past week; if Katherine had been disdainful, the girl Huguette had been kind, and the Golden Scull had found the dainty soldier a frequent visitor. It was Huguette who, after listening to Noel's complaints of the Grand Constable, had suggested to him, in apparent artlessness of heart,that he could play upon the king's superstitions through a new astrologer and had promised to find him a star-gazer who would say anything and everything that Messire Noel wished to have said. The scheme had appealed to Noel, and this very evening he expected Huguette to bring the astrologer to him, to which end he had entrusted her with a password which would admit strangers into the royal garden.

As he mused, a figure in a pilgrim's gown came cautiously out of the shadows into the moonlight behind him and stood for a moment watching him. The god Pan could see the face that smiled under the pilgrim's hood - a girl's face, with bright eyes framed in golden hair, but when the girl saw Noel, she slipped a mask over her face, drew her pilgrim's gown closely about her slim body, and tip-toed lightly across the grass to touch Noel on the shoulder.

Noel turned with a start, and faced, as he believed, a masquerading palmer.

"May I vend you a benevolence, gentleman?" Huguette asked, disguising her voice in an unfamiliar gruffness.

Noel waved aside importunacy.

"Pass your ways, pilgrim. I am in no mood for motley."

He turned away, but the persistent pilgrim followed him.

"Are you in a maid's mood, or a mood for a maid?"

Noel stopped impatiently.

"Are you pander as well as pilgrim? I wait for a woman."

The pilgrim's pertinacity was not to be baffled.

"Is she tall or short, young or old, dark or fair, sweet or sour?"

Noel answered whimsically:

"She is of the colour of the chameleon, of the age of the ancient world, of the height of any man's heart, and as bitter-sweet as a crushed quince."

The girl pulled off her mask and threw back her hood.

"Is she of my feet, favour, years and savour?"

The moment he saw her face Noel gave a cry of delight.

"You are welcome, witch," he shouted, "for you. bring the best love in the world!"

He sprang to catch the girl in his arms, but she repulsed him gently.

"Hush! I am no love-monger now, no gallantry girl, but a most politic plotter. The world spins like a potter's wheel to shape the vessel of our enterprise. We have a wizard ready for your king. Will Louis come?"

Noel nodded decisively.

"As linnet to looking-glass. He is greedy of star-wisdom. Does your astrologer know his lesson?"

"He is parrot-perfect. When all is quiet, give an owl's cry thrice, and a friend will bring him. He will warn the king against his Grand Constable; he will praise Tristan, applaud Olivier, and commend Messire Noel le Jolys."

Noel chuckled.

"Then I shall be king of the castle, and you shall have a great gold chain and pearls as big as a virgin's tears."

Noel did not detect the scorn in Huguette's voice, as she answered with apparent amiability:

"You know the way to win a woman."

"I am no jingling rhyme-broker, I thank heaven!" Noel cried. "I pay my way."

He caught Huguette in his arms as he spoke and sought to kiss her, but she avoided him dexterously.

"I will kiss you when you win," she cried.

Noel would have pushed his suit further, but at that moment the great clock of the palace chimed the half-hour and struck upon his memory as well as upon his ear. He knew that the king expected him and he abandoned his love-making reluctantly.

"You are indeed a politician," he sighed. "I must wait on the king."

He opened the door of the tower and stood for a moment looking regretfully at the girl, who smiled at him temptingly, then he passed in and drew the door behind him.

The moment he had disappeared, the girl's bearing changed. Her face and gesture blazoned a world of contempt for her courtier lover.

"Fool, dunce, dolt, ass, peacock, buzzard, owl!" she stormed. Then her rage faded and she turned sadly on her heel as another man's name came into her heart and fluttered to her lips. "The world is as sour as a rotten orange since François went into exile."

Her glance fell on the lute which lay on the marble seat where Villon had left it. She took it up and began to thrum it pensively, whispering to herself the words of Villon's song:

"Daughters of Pleasure, one and all, Of form and features delicate,"

she murmured to herself. As she did so, Villon, weary of wandering in the rose alleys, came into the moonlit space and saw the cloaked and hooded figure where it sat. In a moment his mind recalled the strange greetings he had overheard between the two pilgrims.

"There is another of those pilgrims," he said to himself, determined now to solve the mystery. He crossed the grass quickly to the figure's side and saluted it.

"Hail, little brother."

Huguette leaped to her feet and answered lightly:

"Hail, little sister."

"Why little sister?" Villon asked in some astonishment.

The masked pilgrim answered him smartly:

"If I am a brother of yours, you must need be a sister of mine. But you talk out of the litany."

"What harm," Villon retorted, "if you give me responses?"

Huguette shrugged her shoulders.

"I will give you no more than good-bye," she said, and turned to leave him, but Villon caught her by the arm.

"You shall not show me your heels till I show myself your face," he insisted.

Before the girl could prevent him, he had flung back her hood and snatched the mask from her face. To his amazement he found himself looking on the fair, familiar face of Huguette, and in astonishment he cried her name. The girl, astounded at being recognized, came close to him.

"Who are you? "she asked.

For answer, Villon unmasked.

Huguette looked closely into his face, at first Without any sign of recognition, then suddenly the knowledge came to her and she caught him in her arms with a cry of joy.

"François, you dear devil, where have you been this thousand years? They said you were banished. How brave you are! Where did you steal so much splendour? Are you cutting purses? Are you plucking mantles?"

Villon tried to stay her questions.

"What are you doing here, Abbess?"

"The fair fool Noel has taken a week-long fancy to me, and I am making an age-long fool of him. Kiss me," she urged, putting her face very near to Villon's. Villon drew back his head.

"You should keep your kisses for the fair fool Noel."

Huguette drew away from him angrily.

"When you were as lean as a cat and as ragged as a sparrow, you were not so nice a precisian. Has some great lady bewitched you? Can you only woo in silk and win in velvet? If the kernel be sweet, what does the husk matter? Heaven's pity! Why should a woman love you?"

Villon took no notice of her petulance but repeated his question:

"What are you doing here, Abbess?"

The girl's rage was as short as a summer's shower. She turned again to him, fondling him.

"Well, I cannot shut the door of my heart in your smooth face. Ren de Montigny has a great game afoot, and you are back in time to share in it."

"What game?" Villon asked.

Huguette answered:

"The fair fool Noel, advised by me, has persuaded the king to see an astrologer here to-night when the gardens are quiet. Noel believes that the astrologer will advise the king to fling his Grand Constable out of the window and call Messire Noel in at the door, but the comrades of the cockleshell really mean much more mischief. When once we get the king within reach of our fingers, we mean to snap him up and carry him out of Paris, willy nilly, and sell him to the Duke of Burgundy."

Villon caught his breath.

"A great game!" he cried. "But who is this astrologer?"

"Thibaut d'Aussigny," she answered, "who pretends to be dead, but who lives for this revenge."

Villon leaped to his feet. He remembered what Katherine thought she had seen.

"Then it was he!" he said.

Huguette went on with her story.

"Noel is to give us the signal by crying an owl's cry thrice."

Villon was revolving many thoughts in his mind and he hardly heeded her.

"This adventure of the astrologer might be turned to

my advantage. Here is a chance in a thousand," he muttered to himself, as he paced restlessly on the grass. "I have but to close my eyes and shut my ears and the good Thibaut carries the good Louis to the good Burgundy to-night, and there can be no hanging to-morrow."

The girl followed after him, catching at his sleeve to stay him.

"What are you talking about?"

Villon went on, unheeding her, whispering to himself:

"If they cut Gaffer Louis' throat between them, the world were rid of a crooked-witted king, and I free to win Katherine, hold Paris, be the first man in France - "

"François, speak to me," Huguette pleaded, but she pleaded in vain.

"One would say I were a fool to let such occasion slip through my ten commandments. But I have learned a thing called honour, which I must not lose for the sake of my lady."

Huguette flung herself in front of him and stopped his restless walk.

"François! François!"

"Yes, child, yes."

"What does it matter to you what they do with the fool king?"

"Abbess, I must have a finger in this pie. Abbess, for the old sake's sake, will you keep me a secret?"

The girl looked up at him lovingly.

"I will always do your bidding."

"I have a mind to play my part in this enterprise. I am the king of the Cockleshells and I have returned to authority. Give me your pilgrim's gown, girl, and mind, not a word to the brotherhood. I want to take friend Thibaut by surprise."

As he spoke, he pulled off the pilgrim's gown, and Huguette stood before him in her familiar boy's dress of green.

"Hide among the roses until the sport begins," he cried.

The girl flung her arms about him.

"Dear François!" she cried, and then ran swiftly away from him and disappeared into the rose-scented night.

Villon looked after the girl as she ran.

"The girl is as fleet as a hare and as wild witted," he said to himself. Then he flung Huguette from his thoughts and faced the great problem.

"How does the balance go?" he asked himself, and he weighed the air with his hands as if their cups held the precious things he spoke of.

"In the one hand, a great king's life; in the other, a poor poet's honour. King, beggar, beggar, king."

He paused a moment, looking down the long lane of infinite possibilities. He owed nothing to Louis after all. Louis had made him the plaything of a shameless trick; had thrust honour upon him in mockery; had tantalized him with a dream of a dream. Ere another sunset, if a woman's heart were not his for the winning, he would be swinging, grisly enough, with his tongue through his teeth, and the ravens wheeling about his ears, upon the Paris gallows. It was but to let Thibaut d'Aussigny play out his play and snare the old black fox, and then Villon had Paris to himself, was absolved from all penalty, might in the light of the new love the people had for him, do, or at least try to do, pretty much as he pleased with the kingless kingdom. It was a dazzling prospect.

"Why not?" he asked himself. Then, in a moment, the reasons why not rose up against him - not to be cheated, not to be banished. He had given his word; he had sworn fealty to the fantastic monarch who had played with him and to whom he owed at least the - realization of great dreams and the golden chance of winning his heart's desire. He had given his word. That would not have meant much to him eight days ago when he lived in a sick atmosphere of lies and dodges and tricks and meannesses, where the lips were as ready to deceive as the fingers to filch, and where a successful falsehood was almost as much applauded as a successful theft. But now, as he had said, he had learned a thing called honour; the whole meaning of life had been changed for him in the sunshine of a fair girl's favour, and what was but yesterday possible, probable, even pleasant, was to-day surely impossible. He murmured her name to himself - "Katherine!" - as a charm against horrible temptation, and his heart strengthened under the spell.

He turned to enter the tower, but as he did so the tower door was pushed out against him and he found himself face to face with Noel le Jolys. Noel started in astonishment at the sight of his rival, but Villon caught him by the wrist. The poor popinjay was too brave a bird to be Thibaut d'Aussigny's decoy-duck.

"Messire Noel," he said; "I have a word to say; in your ear," and he drew him inside the tower and stood with him for a moment in the darkness, whispering speech that made Noel's pulse beat fast. Then Villon left him and sped swiftly up the winding stairs that led to the king's room, while Noel, left alone, pushed open the door again and passed out into the garden, his head dizzy with strange news. Placing his hands like a shell about his mouth, he gave the cry of an owl three times with a little interval between each cry, and then softly withdrew again into the tower, and in his turn raced with a throbbing heart up the narrow steps that led to the king's chamber.

CHAPTER X

UNDER WHICH KING?

The rose garden seemed to be as quiet as a church-yard. No sound was heard save the faint soughing of the evening wind among the rose bushes, no sight resembling humanity visible save the face of Pan looking down mockingly upon the crimson blossoms that girdled him. Yet in a few seconds it became plain that the god Pan was not the only occupant of the garden. Through quiet alleyways, cloaked and cowled figures came stealing, six in number - men with pilgrims' cloaks about their shoulders, and pilgrims' hoods upon their heads - men who carried cockleshells upon the sleeves of their gabardines - all converging through the dark walks of the garden to a common centre, and that centre the grassy space before the king's watch tower. The six figures huddled together at the base of the image of Pan. One of them who seemed to be their leader, a man of giant form, spoke, and the voice was the voice of Thibaut d'Aussigny.

"Are we all here?" he asked.

The nearest pilgrim to him answered with the voice of René de Montigny.

"Aye, and ready to gather the royal rose of this garden."

As he spoke there came a faint click at the latch of the tower door. Thibaut waved his companions apart.

"Keep close," he said, and four of the pilgrim forms disappeared swiftly into the spaces of shadow. Only Thibaut and René remained, standing masked and attentive, their eyes fixed upon the tower door. It opened and Noel le Jolys emerged, followed by, the slight, hunched figure in faded black velvet for whom the eyes of the conspirators were so eager. Noel advanced questioning:

"Is the star-gazer here?"

René de Montigny answered him glibly as a showman patters the praise of his wares.

"Aye. He is the wonder of the world. He can read the stars more easily than a tapster the score on his shutter. He can spell you the high luck and the low. Bohemian, Egyptian, Arabian wisdom have no mysteries for him."

As René ceased, the royal figure with a sweeping gesture of his hand made a sign of dismissal to Noel, who bowed respectfully and withdrew into the tower. The king then beckoned to the mighty figure in the palmer's weed, and Thibaut advanced slowly until he was within touch of his prey, when he suddenly flung out his great hand and caught his enemy by the throat, gripping him into silence while his right hand bared and brandished a dagger. The figure in black dropped under his grasp, trembled and gasped, but the hand of Thibaut was too strong upon him and he could not speak or cry out. Thibaut hissed at him:

"Sire, I can decipher your destiny. Do not speak or I will kill you!"

He pressed the point of the dagger close to the captive's neck and smiled to see him shudder.

"I am Thibaut d'Aussigny, sire, whom you thought to be dead, but who lives to prison you."

As he spoke his companions emerged from the gloom and gathered around Thibaut and the king, a little menacing circle of determined men.

"You are in the toils. Silent you are still a man; give tongue and you are simple carrion. You must come to the knees of Burgundy. You shall be the Duke's footstool!"

The cowering black figure wriggled and quivered as if every one of Thibaut's words were a stroke of a whip that cut into his flesh; his eager hands clawed piteously at Thibaut's grasping arm, until his very agony of terror aroused the contempt of his captor. He pushed the king from him contemptuously, and the king dropped on the ground a black and helpless heap of fear.

"Can a king be such a cur? Burgundy won't hurt you if you do as he bids you. I won't hurt you if you do as I bid you."

The black figure rocked, a pitiable bundle of terrors, apparently sobbing plaintively. Thibaut sickened at such shameless fear.

"Stop crying," he growled.

René de Montigny, who had been watching keenly the actions of the prisoner, interrupted:

"He seems to be laughing," he said.

Thibaut gave a cry of astonishment and stooped down over the prostrate man, who greeted him with a prolonged and hearty peal of laughter, which staggered the giant like a blow in the face. At that moment the tower door was flung open and Tristan appeared.

"The king!" he cried in a voice of thunder.

In another moment, as if by magic, the little garden space was girdled by the archers of the Scottish Guard, strong hands made sure of the baffled conspirators, and to their astonishment Louis himself made his appearance through the open doorway, his malign face smiling in the moonlight.

Justin Huntly McCarthy

CHAPTER XI

THE DEATH OF A WANTON

The sham king leaped to his feet, still laughing, flung off the black cap with its little row of leaden saints and the rusty black mantle which mimicked the king's habit, and stood delighted and defiant before Thibaut, the François Villon who thus a second time had crossed his path.

"Well, friend, what has the wizard told you?" Louis asked blandly.

Villon swayed with laughter as he pointed to the bewildered giant.

"Wonders, sire," he answered. "I have not laughed so heartily since I attained greatness." But even as he spoke Thibaut had recovered his wits. He might be defeated but he would not be unavenged.

"You shall laugh no more!" he shouted, wrenching himself free from restraint, and he sprang at his enemy with lifted dagger.

From behind the shadow of the statue of Pan there came a warning shriek, and swiftly between Villon and Thibaut a slim green figure darted and slim green arms clasped Villon around the neck. The dagger of Thibaut drove deep into the soft body of Huguette.

With a curse Thibaut turned and, sweeping aside the archers who tried to stop him, disappeared down the nearest alley. Noel le Jolys, drawing his sword, rushed in pursuit, followed by several soldiers. Villon held the bleeding body of the girl in his arms, and tried his best to stanch the wound which was staining the green jerkin a dull red, but the girl protested faintly, pushing his ministering hand away.

"Let me alone; I am done for," she gasped.

Olivier was by her side in an instant, eyeing the wound with the professional interest of the surgeon-barber and looking from it to the girl's pale face. Villon's gaze questioned him. Olivier shrugged his shoulders and shook his head. Villon knew that the wound was mortal, and his own blood seemed like water within him. He carried the girl across the grass to the marble seat and rested her on it, the red stain on the green coat growing wider and wider as they moved.

"Courage, Abbess, courage, lass," he whispered, fighting with his horror and his sorrow as he moaned to himself: "That any one should die for me!"

The girl's arms clung closer about his neck and her lips moved faintly. He stooped close to her to catch her words.

"This is a strange end, François. I always thought I should die in a bed. Here is another kind of battlefield. Give me drink."

"Some water," Villon cried to Olivier, who stood a little apart from the pair with the resigned look of the physician who knows that his art is of no avail.

Huguette protested faintly.

"Not water. Wine. I have ever loved the taste of it, and 'tis too late to change now."

Olivier filled a cup from the flagon on the table and was for lifting it to the girl's lips, but her feeble hand repulsed him and she pleaded to Villon:

"Give it to me, François."

Villon took the cup from the barber's hand, lifted it to the dying girl's lips, and she drank greedily. The strong wine gave her for a moment something of its own false strength, and she struggled to her feet, Villon rising with her and supporting her.

"Your health, François. I suppose I have been a great sinner. Will God forgive me?"

Villon stifled a heavy groan, but he was sworn to console her if he could, and, indeed, he believed his words of consolation.

"He understands his children."

The heavy head drooped its golden curls upon his shoulder.

"You always were hopeful," she said brokenly. Then suddenly clasping him tightly, she cried: "Many men have taken my body; only you ever took my heart.

Give me your lips."

Villon's spirit was troubled. It seemed to him that his lips were bound to wait for that kiss of his lady's, and yet the dying girl loved him and he had loved the dying girl after a fashion, and he could not refuse her now. He bent to grant her prayer, when suddenly she shook herself free from his arms and began to sing faintly the words of the song he had made for her:

"Daughters of Pleasure, one and all,

Then she caught her breath with a sob and slipped to the last lines of the verse:

"Use your red lips before too late, Love ere love flies beyond recall."

She shook her head back in a wild peal of laughter: then she gave a great cry and fell forward. Villon caught her, looked in her face and knew that she was dead, and that the best of his old bad life lay dead with her.

Olivier in obedience to an order of the king's, gave a signal and the girl's body was swiftly wrapped in a soldier's cloak and laid gently upon a pair of crossed halberds. As this was being done, Noel le Jolys came panting back with a red sword in his hand.

"Thibaut d'Aussigny is dead, sire," he said; "my hand was the hand that finished him."

Then as his eyes fell on the dead body, they shone with sudden tears. Villon went up to him and touched him on the shoulder.

"I leave this dead woman in your hands," he said, "for I think you had a kindness for her. See that she has Christian burial."

Noel bowed his head and followed in silence the girl's body. The garden was left to Louis and Villon, Tristan and Olivier, and the handful of captured rogues who stood apart, strongly guarded and stripped of their pilgrims' garb, gazing amazed at Louis and his double. Villon, silent too, looked after the little group that bore away the dead girl's body. His mind was a warfare of wild memories. Strange recollections of times and places with Huguette came crowding up and beating piteously upon his brain. He thought of what he had been, and groaned; of what he was now, and his soul cried out as in prayer in the name of Katherine.

CHAPTER XII

A VIRGIN'S TEARS

The king's hand fell upon his shoulder and shattered his meditations.

"Are you so dashed by the death of a wanton?" the king asked mockingly.

Villon turned upon him in a noble rage.

"She had God's breath in her body, sire," he said. Then drawing his hand across his forehead as if to dissipate the sad fancies that oppressed him, he went on:

"I have been John-a-Nods for the moment, sire; now I am Jack-a-Deeds again. The hour for battle is at hand."

Louis shrugged his shoulders.

"You have done me a good turn, gossip," he said, "and may ask any grace of me except your life. That depends on your lady."

Villon looked over at the corner where his old boon companions were huddled together, the miserable centre of a circle of soldiers.

Justin Huntly McCarthy

"Sire," he said; "grant me the lives of those rascals. They shall ride with me and fight for France to-night. It is better than making them play bob-apple on the evil tree."

The king whispered a few words to Tristan, and Tristan very reluctantly gave the order of liberation. The comrades of the Cockleshell were freed of their bonds and bade to stand apart, under guard and out of earshot, to wait on destiny for future commands. At this moment Louis, glancing upwards, caught sight between the flower vases on the terrace of a gleam of crimson, the crimson silk of a woman's robe. It betrayed the presence of Katherine de Vaucelles, who had come hard upon the hour of nine to seek for her lover, but who paused irresolute at the head of the stairs, noting the presence of the king. Louis beckoned to her amicably, and she began slowly to descend the staircase. Louis came over to Villon and whispered in his ear:

"Here comes your lady. I think your love-fruit is ripe and you need not stand on tip-toe to pick it."

Villon answered him with burning eyes:

"Sire, I believe I have won the rose of the world."

Louis chuckled like an enraptured raven.

"The Count of Montcorbier is luckier than François Villon. But the lady has a high mind and a fierce spirit. She may not relish the deception, pardon the cheat his lie!"

Something in the king's words struck upon Villon's

fiery hopes like a stream of ice-cold water and seemed to quench them. He was like a man who, long playing at blind-man's-buff, suddenly has the bandage plucked from his eyes and stands dazzled and blinking in the sunlight. After all, he was not the Count of Montcorbier; after all, he was not the Grand Constable of France; after all, he was only a masquerading beggar who had won the heart of a lady under false colours; who had triumphed by flying a false flag. In all those seven splendid days this simple thought had never come to him. His whole soul had been so taken captive by the fascination of the part he had been permitted to play that he forgot he was playing a part, and allowed his fancy to believe that a week-long dream would endure forever. Now he knew himself and what he had done and what he must do. A divine farce had turned to sudden tragedy. He turned to the king with a groan.

"Cheat, lie," he repeated. "Sire, those words fling me from my fool's paradise. Kill me if I fail to win her, but I will tear this mask from my face, this falsehood from my heart."

Louis grinned at him.

"Please yourself. Win her or swing. Either way contents me."

As he spoke, he turned away. Katherine had descended the steps and was moving across the grass to greet her hero, who stood with clasped hands in the moonlight like a man struck dumb. Katherine was carrying in her hands a crimson scarf fringed with gold, and she lifted it to him as she spoke.

"Wear this with my prayers. With it, I give you my hand and heart. You shall carry my plighted troth with you into the battle. Let me tell my love to all the world."

Swiftly and lightly she threw it about his neck before he could find words, but now he spoke:

"Wait, wait! You must say no more until you know me."

The girl's eyes widened with surprise.

"Do I not know you?"

Villon thrust his face forward very close to hers.

"Look into my face," he said. "Look well. Do you see nothing there that reminds you of other hours?"

Katherine smiled divinely.

"Of happy hours in this rose garden."

Villon insisted fiercely:

"No, no! Of a dark night, a tavern, a cloaked woman, a sordid fellow dreaming sottishly by the fire, a prayer, a love-tale and a promise, a crowd of bullies and wantons, a quarrel, a fight with sword and lantern in the dark, a breast knot of ribbon flung from a gallery - "

Katherine recoiled a little, with a horror in her eyes.

"What are you trying to tell me?" she asked.

Villon dropped on his knees with a groan.

"Here is the knot of ribbon which you flung to me in the Fircone Tavern. Oh, pity me! I am François Villon."

Katherine pressed her hands to her forehead.

"I can hear what you say, but it makes no mark on my brain."

Villon's words ran fast from him:

"I am François Villon and yet no longer he, for my old evil self is dead. I am François Villon who served you with his sword, who praised you with his pen, and who loves you with all his soul."

The girl's whole body shook with fear as she answered:

"It isn't true! It isn't true! I don't believe you."

Villon sprang to his feet.

"Whatever my fate is," he cried, "you shall know the truth."

Turning to where the released conspirators stood apart, he called to them peremptorily:

"Guy! Eene! All of you, come here!"

Amazed to be thus summoned in their own names by so great a personage as the Grand Constable of France, the thieves crept forward timidly and, in obedience to Villon's commanding gestures, gathered about him as he turned to them, pressing his face near to their faces, and cried:

"Look at me closer - closer. Don't you know François Villon in spite of this new spirit shining in his eyes?"

René de Montigny gave a cry of recognition.

"I should never have known you. You are so strangely changed."

Guy Tabarie endorsed him.

"Still,'tis his dear old countenance."

Katherine watching the scene in sick despair, turned piteously to the king.

"Sire, sire, is this true?"

Louis, who had been watching all with unmitigated satisfaction, answered fleeringly:

"Most true, pretty mistress. You disdained me for this."

With blazing eyes and trembling hands Katherine moved across the grass to where Villon stood.

"Pitiful traitor, why did you live this lie?"

Villon pleaded desperately:

"I loved you."

Katherine's anger flamed into a great fire.

"Do not shame the sweet word. I hate you! To think the face that I have learned to love should mask so base a heart!"

Then as Villon drew a little closer to her, in an agony of entreaty, she struck out at him with both hands, beating him on the breast in an unconquerable fury. Villon bowed beneath the blow while she raged at him:

"You have stolen my love like a thief, you have crucified my pride. I hate you! Go back to the dregs and lees of life, skulk in your tavern, forget, what I shall never forget, that so base a thing as you ever came near me!"

The king was by her side in an instant and whispering into her ear:

"Is this the course of true love?"

She swung upon him in scorn.

"Sire, you have wreaked a royal revenge upon a woman. There are no tears in my eyes yet, but I pray they will come that I may weep myself clean of this memory."

With clasped hands and set lips she moved away from Louis and stood apart in the moonlight, a fixed and rigid figure of despair. Louis stepped to where Villon stood in stricken anguish and whispered to him:

"I am afraid you will hang to-morrow, Master Villon."

Villon threw back his head defiantly.

"I should be glad to greet the gallows now, but I have a deed to do before I die."

As he spoke the great bell of the palace beat out the first stroke of the hour of nine. It roused the wounded spirit in his soul. He moved to where Katherine stood and spoke to her:

"I dreamed that love through which I have been born again could lift me to your lips. The dream is over. But you bade me serve France, and I ride and fight for you to-night."

While he spoke the Lords of Lau, of Eiviere and of Nantoillet in panoply of war came from the palace with their immediate followers. The garden began to fill with the picked men of the enterprise hurrying on the summons of the warning bell to follow their leader on his sortie. Villon's pages brought the armour of the Grand Constable and began to buckle it upon him. While this was being done, he turned and spoke to his brothers-in-arms:

"Comrades, let each man carry himself to-night as if the fate of France depended upon his heart, his arm, his courage. Strike for the mothers that bore you, the wives that comfort you, the children that Renéw you - the women that love you." For a moment his voice quailed and almost failed him. There were happy men there, no doubt, whom women loved. But he rallied in a breath and his voice rang out valiantly again: "Forward in God's name and the king's!"

And every soldier present echoed him: "Forward in God's name and the king's!"

CHAPTER XIII

THE REDE OF FIVE RIDING ROGUES

Through the silent streets of Paris a slender line of steel moved slowly - the thread of which Master François Villon was the needle pricked to sew the realm of France together. The Grand Constable rode at the head with the Lords of Lau, of Riviere, and of Nantoillet, and somewhere at the tail rode the five released rascals and babbled beneath their breaths as they rode. For the order to keep silence did not count until the gates of Paris were reached and began to turn on their hinges to let Villon's adventurers forth. Every man of the ruffians had a stout sword swinging at his girdle; every man of them sported a steel cap upon his head; every man of them felt his heart pulsing with rare emotions and his brain busy with strange thoughts. René de Montigny spoke first the thing that filled his mind.

"It must be a devil of a business," he reflected, "to be bullied like that by a beauty. Blood, but she is beautiful, and blood, but she can bellow."

Guy Tabarie chuckled fatly. "I have been bullied so many times by grey-faced drabs that I would take my trouncing patiently from such a pair of lips. It was meat and drink to look at her and think thoughts."

Jehan le Loup frowned sourly. "Had I been Master François and black Louis not been by I should have tried to mend my luck with a cudgel. At best and worst she would have had something to curse for after a lusty thumping."

Casin Cholet licked his lips. "I shall think of her," he said, "when next I meet with a sweetheart. With a little wit your honest rascal can be as happy as a king. In the dark all fur is of the same colour."

Oolin de Cayeulx yawned. "What are we going a-riding for?" he questioned. "I would sooner have stayed in the king's rose garden and filled my belly as we did last week when the great lord in gold tissue pitied us. And to think that it was no more than François after all! I could jam my dagger between his shoulder-blades for making such a ninny of me."

"I knew him all the time," Guy Tabarie was beginning when René de Montigny silenced him with a ringing clip on the nearest ear which nearly unsaddled the fat rogue. "You lie, Mountain, you lie," he whispered. "Do you think that if he cheated me your pig's eyes could read the riddle? No, no, he fooled us fairly and he fooled us well, but he treated us kindly and we can afford to cry quits."

"A strange thing," mused Colin, "that a trifle of hair less on a man's chin and a trifle of dirt less on a man's cheek, with some matter of clean linen and a smooth jerkin, can make such a difference."

"Not at all," said René de Montigny," we are all the same at the core, every man-jack and woman-jill of us, hungering, thirsting, lusting, just after the same fashion. 'Tis only the coat that counts."

"'Tis you who lie now," grunted Tabarie. "There's no gold tissue in the world that would make you as cunning as François. You would never have done as he did if the king had made you the pick of the litter."

Rend whistled through his teeth. "May be so, may be not," he said. "No man can tell what he may do till he is given his chance to test his mettle. Oh opportunity, golden opportunity! If I were François Villon I would shape an image of gold in your name and praise you for a saint."

"I wonder what that girl will say," mused Tabarie, "if our François comes back with the Duke of Burgundy in his pocket!"

"I wonder what she will say," sneered Jehan le Loup, "if he trundles back feet foremost with a hole in his body and half a head."

"Whatever happens is sure to vex her," said Casin Cholet. "Women are made that way."

"Our poor minions will be lonely to-night," said Colin.

"I doubt it," said René de Montigny drily, and then he sighed a little. "Poor Abbess!"

Sudden tears smeared Tabarie's fat cheeks.

"She was a brave wench if ever," he snivelled. "Through wellfare or illfare she was always the same, and would share board and blanket with a friend though his pouch were as barren as Sarah's body."

"It was ten thousand pities," said Eene, "that she fell so love-sick for François. Did he give her some philtre, some elixir, do you think? François is a fine fellow though, I'll not deny it, but he's had the devil's own luck, and by our patron St. Nicholas there be others as fine as he."

As he spoke the great gate of the city yawned noiselessly, and stealthy and silent the hope of Paris glided into the darkness and was swallowed up by the night.

CHAPTER XIV

THE BANNERS OF BURGUNDY

The yellow dawn, rippling over Paris, found her streets strangely silent, strangely quiet. A few good citizens were abed, but most good citizens were abroad on that kindly June morning, for there was business doing outside the walls of Paris which tempted every man inside the walls to those walls, and that business was the battle that was raging, and had raged since nightfall, between the troops of King Louis on one side under the Grand Constable of France, and the troops of the Duke of Burgundy and his allies on the other. Paris might have been that strange city of slumber told of by the wanderer in the Arabian tale, or that poppied palace where the sleeping beauty and her court lay waiting the coming of the hero. If Asmodeus whisking his way on the wings of the wind with any astonished travelling companion in tow had paused over Paris and unroofed it for the benefit of his fellow-voyager, most of the rooms would have been found as empty as the streets.

But there was one spot in the city - an open place by the river, between an ancient gate and the church of the Celestins - which was alive and busy with a strange activity of its own. It was empty enough and the windows of its houses stared vacantly upon its

Justin Huntly McCarthy

emptiness, but there were two men in possession of its tranquillity who had been toiling hard at a singular piece of work. They were putting the finishing touches to the erection of a tall, gaunt gallows with its steps and platform, which occupied a space midway between the gateway and the grey old Gothic church. In curious contrast to the sinister grimness of the gibbet, there rose opposite to it on the side of the church a dais, richly draped with royal velvet, splendidly spangled with fleur-de-lis and brave with armourial bearings.

The two men who were working at the gallows having finished their job, came out into the open space and stretched themselves. One was a tall, thin, grave, poplar-tree of a man, clad in sad-coloured clothes and conspicuous for a long rosary of enormous beads which he carried around his neck and which from time to time he handled with ostentatious sanctimony. The other was as complete a contrast to his companion as could be desired by the humorous painter. He was a plump, spry little fellow, brightly dressed and bubbling over with merry, roguish spirits, which formed the most fantastic foil to the lugubriousness of his fellow-worker. Any good citizen of Paris, arising belated, if any such there may have been, and hurrying to the walls to know how things went for the king's cause, would have recognized readily enough in these two strange opposites two of the most dreaded of the myrmidons of Tristan l'Hermite, no less than his two chief hangmen, Trois-Echelles and Petit-Jean. Trois-Echelles was the long, cadaverous hangman; Petit-Jean was the stout, droll hangman, but when it came to a push and a pinch, both were hangmen and hung in the same manner, if not with the same manners. Petit-Jean pulled a flagon of wine from under the platform of the gallows, lifted it to his lips, drained a mighty draught, sighed with satisfaction, and held out the bottle to his brother craftsman.

"Drink and be merry."

Trois-Echelles, making gestures of protestation with his head but taking the bottle with his hand none the less, drew a deep draught from its throttle and sighed as sadly as his friend sighed gladly.

"I will drink but I cannot be merry. What's the good of building a noble gallows if nobody looks at it? One might as well be building a church."

Petit-Jean laughed good-naturedly.

"All Paris is on the walls watching the battle. Lucky Paris!"

Trois-Echelles laughed ill-humoredly.

"Not so lucky if we don't win the battle."

Petit-Jean was complacent.

"Whichever wins will need us to hang the losers. Look at the bright side, man."

Trois-Echelles fumbled his beads furtively.

"I've lost heart, I tell you. I haven't hanged a man for a week."

As he mourned over this melancholy retrospect, the door of a little house hard by the church opened and an old woman, propping herself on a crutch stick, came hobbling slowly across the open space towards the church. Petit-Jean knew her well enough, for they both lodged in the same house and both on the same floor of attics. He knew she was the mother of the greatest scapegrace in all Paris, a rascal named François Villon, who had disappeared, Heaven alone knew where, to the old lady's great despair. He saluted her good humoredly.

"Good morrow to your nightcap, mother. Have you found your lost sheep?"

Mother Villon shook her head wistfully.

"They say he is banished, but he has sent me money, bless him! though I touch none of it, lest it be badly come by."

Trois-Echelles stopped fumbling his beads and advanced towards her, extending his hand.

"Give it to me to spend on masses?" he asked sanctimoniously.

Petit-Jean danced between them.

"Lend it to me for drink money," he urged.

The old woman paid no heed to their proposals. Her tired eyes had caught sight of the grim structure in wood which usurped a place in a familiar scene. She shaded her eyes and peered at it, asking:

"For whom do you build this gallows?"

The glum hangman answered gloomily:

"Oddly enough, we don't know. 'Make me a gallows here,' says the Constable, 'in the open place, and sieges for the king and his courtiers.'"

Mother Villon, her simple curiosity easily satisfied, dropped her informant a curtsey and hobbled slowly up the steps into the church.

Petit-Jean stretched himself again and yawned.

"I'll to sleep and dream of hanging a king."

Trois-Echelles put a lean finger to his lean chin.

"Treason, friend, if Tristan heard you."

Petit-Jean's eyes twinkled.

"Well, let's say an archbishop," he said.

Trois-Echelles nodded approvingly.

"An archbishop ought to make a good end."

His mind pleased itself with the picture of so high a dignitary of the church in his full canonicals coming under his tender care and being exhorted by his pious counsels.

The two hangmen climbed on the platform of the grisly erection, and, calmly indifferent to the nature of their bed, were in a few moments fast asleep and snoring as merrily as if every man in the world had been hung and there was nothing else for them to do but to take it easy for the rest of their days.

The hard weariness of work and the easy weariness of wine had made them so heavy-headed that their slumbers were not disturbed by the sound of footfalls, though the footfalls echoed strangely loud in the lonely deserted place-the footfalls of a woman, swift and impatient, the footfalls of a man swiftly pursuing. In another moment the woman and the man came into the open space, now bright and shining with the risen sun. The woman was Katherine de Vaucelles; the man was Noel le Jolys.

As Katherine entered the silent square, she paused for a moment a few paces from the church, and turning, looked at her silent follower.

"Why do you follow me?" she asked, and Noel le Jolys, who had dogged her footsteps from the palace, answered her briskly:

"You should not walk unguarded. Therefore I shadow you."

Katherine scorned him.

"You may well play the shadow, for you cast no shadow of your own. The streets are very idle - the streets are very quiet. I would sooner have my loneliness than your company. Let me pass to my prayers." For Noel had glided between her and the church, and stood barring her passage deferentially.

"For your lover?" he asked, and Katherine flashed at him:

"You have a small mind to ask, yet I have a great mind to answer. My prayers are for a brave gentleman whom

I shall never see again."

As she spoke, the cup of her heart seemed to run over with red tears, and the bitter waters trembled in her eyes. Her thoughts wandered over the long white night and her sleepless sorrow, and her vigil by the window, looking out into the rose garden, and her tired eyes straining in vain through the dark for any sight, and her tired ears straining in vain for any sound of the battle in which the lord of her heart was risking his life. For she knew it now; she had learned it through those age-long hours of agony, that he whom she called her enemy was the lord of her heart, that in spite of all her rage at the cheat that had been put upon her, she loved, not the great noble who had done so much to save France - no, nor the ragged poet who had lent her his sword-arm and his sword, but just the man, by whatever name he might be called and in whatever way of life his wheel of fortune might spin, whose hand had proved to be of the right size to hold her heart in its hollow. The Katherine of yesterday seemed to be dead and buried, to have died a fiery death of fierce thoughts, fierce agonies, fierce exultations, and from that travail a new Katherine had come into being with cleansed eyes to see the world truly and with a cleansed soul to know a great soul's truth.

Noel watched her silence but it meant nothing to him, and he tripped into her high thoughts cheerfully.

"I am a brave gentleman," he said, patting himself approvingly upon the breast. "I slew Thibaut d'Aussigny last night. The king has taken me back into favour. If I played the fool's part yesterday, I can play the wise man's part to-morrow. I was a bubble and a gull and a dunce, if you like, but I meant no harm to

Justin Huntly McCarthy

the king, and the king smiles on me. Cannot you do the like?"

Katherine came out of her dream and stood upon the earth again, and disdained him.

"No, for you envy a great spirit and your envy makes you a base thing."

Noel protested pettishly:

"He is no man-angel. He is made of Adam's clay like the rest of us."

Katherine's thoughts had wandered away from her escort; her mind's eyes were busy with waving banners, the shock of meeting lances, the glitter of steel coats and the beating of steel upon steel. Through all the melley, her fancy spied one shining figure in bright armour like, so it seemed to her, Archangel Michael or Archangel Gabriel, riding in the pride of the fight with a smile on his lips, sorrow in his heart, and a token of white ribbon between his breast-plate and his breast.

She answered, not Noel's words, but her thoughts:

"My pride has the right to hate him, but I think he is still my soul's man."

Noel was about to speak again, when he suddenly fell back and doffed his bonnet. Perched on the steps of the church stood the stooped sable figure of the king, just coming from his matinal devotions. In the shadow behind him stood his shadows - Tristan and Olivier.

Katherine, her attention swerved by Noel's glance, turned and swayed a reverence to Louis as he slowly descended the steps. The king surveyed them sardonically.

"Good morning, friends," he said. Then turning to Noel, he ordered, "Take the top of your speed to St. Anthony's gate and bring hot news of the battle."

Noel bowed and sped on his errand. Katherine requested:

"Have I your majesty's leave?"

Tristan and Olivier withdrew themselves discreetly apart, under the shadow of the gallows, that building of all human buildings which was most dear to their hearts and most sacred in their eyes.

Louis came very close to the pale girl and whispered:

"Are you so hungry for your devotions that you cannot waste some worldly words on me? Are you still angry with me for the trick I played on you?"

Katherine's pale face flushed a little as she answered:

"It is wasted spirit to be angry with a king."

Louis grinned.

"You are as pat with your answers as a clerk at matins. Could you give me your heart now if I bent my knee?"

Katherine stifled a great sigh.

"I lost my heart last night; I have not found it again."

Louis flung up his hands in contemptuous amusement.

"The fellow was a fool to blab so glibly. I would have carried the jest farther. But he stood on the punctilio and would not win you without confession."

The girl's heart swelled.

"I am glad he had so much honour," she said, and the shining figure in the bright armour seemed more archangel-like than ever.

Louis looked at her intently, tickling his chin with his forefinger.

"If you wait in the church for his homecoming, you will see how the jest ends," he said.

Katherine made the king a profound reverence and slowly entered the church, every pulse of her body pleading in prayer for her lost lover. She scarcely heeded an old, bowed woman who tottered out, propped on a crutch stick, and who dropped the great lady a respectful curtsey as she passed and went her ways into the silent streets. So the two women in the world whom Villon loved met for the first time.

Louis, left alone, beckoned to Tristan and Olivier, who hurried down to him.

"There goes a brave lady, gossips, a fair lady, a chaste lady. She sails in the high latitudes of lore and deserves to find the Fortunate Islands. Are there not better things to do with Master Villon than to hang him?"

Olivier protested:

"This Villon is such a damnable double dealer that the ass-headed populace loves him better than you."

The king's visage soured.

"That is enough to hang him. Yet I have a kind of liking for the fellow, and my dream troubles me - the star that fell from heaven."

Tristan commented bluffly:

"Hang the rascal while you can and thank heaven you are well rid of him."

Even as he spoke the world seemed suddenly to be full of many noises and many voices. From beyond the gate on the ways that led to the city walls came the clamour of hoarse shouts and cries and the thudding din of running feet. From the other side, from the street that led to the Louvre, came the ordered tramp of soldiers.

Olivier interpreting one interruption, said:

"The people are coming from the walls."

And Tristan interpreted the other.

"The queen, sire," he announced.

Through the narrow space that led into the open square there came a line of soldiers escorting a number of splendidly caparisoned litters - the carriages of the queen and the queen's chief ladies. Louis advanced to the first litter, and extending his hand, assisted the queen to descend and conducted her with an elaborate display of polite affection to the gorgeous dais by the side of the church, where they sat side by side on the small thrones that had been prepared for them. The ladies and gentlemen of the court ranged themselves in their places behind the royal pair and the Scottish archers formed a solid force in front. Through the open gateway came a few running, shouting enthusiasts, outstrippers of the mass of citizens who were returning from the walls. Even the heavy sleep of Trois-Echelles and Petit-Jean was not proof against all this tumult. They awoke, rubbed their eyes, then climbing briskly to their feet, leaned over the platform on the handrails of the gallows and surveyed the scene with interest.

Noel le Jolys pushed his way through the crowd aboat the gateway and advanced to the king.

"Sire," he said, "the latest message from the battle: The day is wholly ours. The Grand Constable returns in triumph. You can hear his music now."

Louis nodded.

"It is very well," he affirmed gravely.

Through the gateway the crowd of people was pouring thick and fast, shouting and cheering and filling the square in front of the dais with a throng of enthusiastic men, women and children, all waving their arms, flinging flowers and yelling welcomes at the topmost pitch of their lungs. The sound of military music and the tramp of marching men could be heard approaching louder and louder.

Five girls had forced their way to the very front row of the throne and were applauding and shouting with the rest. These were the light ladies of the Fircone, Isabeau, Jehanneton, Denise, and Blanche with Guillemette, fat Robin Turgis' fat daughter. They were all in a state of great excitement, for their lovers had vanished over night and their Abbess had disappeared like a dream, and they knew not what had become of them. They had little fear for their lovers, for the good gentlemen of the Fellowship of the Cockleshell had a way of diving into the deep waters of existence at intervals in order to escape the too attentive eye and the too particular finger of the law, and the girls had a vague idea of some great scheme on hand which might easily result in trouble for the brotherhood. As for their Abbess, they were none too sorry to be free from her somewhat decisive authority, and they chattered and babbled like birds escaped from a cage.

By this time the advance guard of the army began to pour in through the narrow mouth of the gateway and to form a line in front of the populace, thus leaving a wide open space between the assembled people and the seated king. From every window heads were thrust and hands extended waving scarfs of silk or scattering flowers. The blare of the soldiers' music grew louder and louder, the tramp of horse and men came nearer and nearer, and then, when the cheering was at its shrillest and the rain of flowers thickest, Villon rode in through the gateway on his great warhorse with his five ruffians close at his heels. Villon's lifted hand gave the signal for a halt and he leaped lightly off his horse and advanced towards the king, a glorious figure to the eyes of the crowd in his shining armour with a scarlet coif upon his helmet. If for a moment his glance rested on the gaunt skeleton of the gallows there came

Justin Huntly McCarthy

no change in the proud composure of his face. Immediately behind him followed the faithful ragamuffins, each of whom bore vivid signs in slung arm, swathed leg or bandaged forehead of the lusty work he had done in the king's name upon the king's enemies. But the slings and swathes and bandages were of no common sort, but splendid bits of silk of many colours, bearing fantastic devices and rich in threads of gold and silver.

As Villon and his fantastic escort strode towards the presence, Noel interposed indignantly. He stretched a pair of protecting arms wide out to ward off from the king the approach of so singular a deputation, while he demanded angrily:

"In heaven's name, sir, who are these scarecrows who flaunt their tatters in the presence of the king?"

The king nursed his chin with an amused smile as Villon answered:

"The scarecrows are rogues who have fought like gentlefolk and these rags are the banners of the enemy."

Even as he spoke the rapscallions stripped the pieces of silk from arm and leg and forehead, shook them out into such semblance of their original shape as battle had left to them and flung them with a gesture of imperial pride on the ground at the foot of the dais.

"Well answered," said Louis regally, while two pursuivants pounced swiftly upon the bits of silk, and gathering them up with reverential fingers, laid them upon the railing in front of the king's chair to be examined with loving care by the queen. Standing erect, Villon addressed the king: "Louis of France, we bring you these silks for your carpet. An hour ago they wooed the wind from Burgundian staves and floated over Burgundian helmets. I will make no vain glory of their winning. Burgundy fought well, but France fought better, and these trophies trail in our triumph. To a mercer's eyes these bits of tissue are but so many squares of damaged web. To a soldier's eye, they cover crowded graves with honour. To a king's eye, they deck one throne with lonely splendour. When we here, who breathe hard from fighting, and ye, who stand there and marvel, are dust, when the king's name is but a golden space in chronicles grey with age, these banners shall hang from Cathedral arches and your children's children's children, lifted in reverent arms, shall peep through the dim air at the faded colours, and baby lips shall whisper an echo of our battle."

CHAPTER XV

THE SHADOW OF THE GALLOWS

As Villon ended a great peal of music came from the church, the magnificent music of a Te Deum Laudamus; while from the soldiers who choked the archway, a glowing sea of steel, there rose one common cry of "God save the Grand Constable!"

Olivier leaned over and whispered to the king;

"They cheer him, sire."

Louis waved him impatiently aside, and leaning over the railing, spoke:

"My Lord Constable, and you, brave soldiers, the King of France thanks you for your gift. Victory was indeed assured you by the justice of our cause. My Lord of Montcorbier, you may promise these brave fellows that their sovereign will remember them."

Swiftly Villon turned and addressed the motley throng behind him:

"In the king's name, a gold coin to every man who fought and a cup of wine to every man, woman and child who wishes to drink the king's health."

The king smiled wryly.

"Ever generous," he said.

"To the end, sire," Villon answered, with an ironic salutation, which Louis answered by an ironic question.

"What have you now to do?"

Villon saluted the king again.

"My latest duty, sire," he answered, and once again he turned to address the multitude:

"Soldiers who have served under me, friends who have fought with me, and you, people, whom I have striven to succour, listen to my amazing swan song. You know me a little as Count of Montcorbier, Grand Constable of France. I know myself indifferently well as François Villon, Master of Arts, broker of ballads and somewhile bibber and brawler. It is now my task as Grand Constable of France to declare that the life of Master François Villon is forfeit and to pronounce on him this sentence, that he be straightway hanged upon yonder gibbet."

His words fell like the beat of a passing bell upon the ears of an absolutely silent crowd and for some few year-long seconds the silence brooded over the place. The five wantons on the fringe of the crowd caught at each others' fingers and gasped. Was that splendid gentleman their old friend, François Villon? As for the five rogues who knew the secret, they had begun to laugh at Villon's first words, but the laughter dried upon their lips as he ended.

From the church suddenly the exultant music of the Te Deum ceased to swell and in its place crept forth upon the silent air the awful notes of a Miserere. The king had been at the ear of the organist that morning and had planned his effects well. The melancholy music stirred the people to murmurs of surprise and protest.

Guy Tabarie, flourishing his notched and bloody sword, thrust his round body forward.

"What jest is this?" he asked.

And Villon answered him:

"Such a jest as I would rather weep over to-morrow than laugh at to-day. For the pitcher breaks at the well's mouth this very morning. Messire Noel, to you I surrender my sword. I like to believe that it has scraped a little shame from its master's coat."

He drew his great war-sword and handed it to Noel le Jolys, who, for one of the few times in his life, astonished into forgetfulness of courtly etiquette, had been staring, open-mouthed, at the astonishing revelation that had just been made to him. The gleam of the war-worn weapon recalled him to himself and he took it from the hands of the doomed man with a grave courtesy which meant something more than the official fulfillment of a formal duty. Noel le Jolys was a soldier and his eyes paid homage to a brave man.

Villon turned to Tristan.

"Master Tristan, perform your office upon this self-doomed felon."

With great alacrity, Tristan moved towards Villon, but his motion was met by such angry murmurs from the crowd, and not from the crowd alone, but from the soldiers who had followed Villon to victory, that even he shrank back instinctively before its menace. There came cries from a thousand throats, calling on the king to pardon the Grand Constable, calling upon those who loved him to rescue him.

"King, is this justice?" René de Montigny, shouted, and his question evoked a roar of approval from the multitude.

The king's keen glance surveyed the scene with no sign of fear and no sign of annoyance. Leaning easily upon the railing, as a man might lean who surveyed an amusing farce or interlude, he addressed the crowd:

"Good people of Paris, you have heard your Grand Constable pronounce sentence upon a criminal. Has Master François Villon any reason to urge, any plea to offer, why the sentence should not be carried out?"

Villon waved his hand disdainfully.

"I have nothing whatever to say, sire. François Villon must die. It's bad luck for him, but he has worse luck and so - to business."

As he spoke he drew near to the line of Scottish archers and two of their number laid hands on him, one at either side. The sight of their hero thus in the very clutch of justice spurred the multitude to Renéwed exasperation. Angry demands for justice, for mercy, for rescue, shook the summer air. Unarmed citizens broke into an armourer's shop hard by, and, seizing whatever weapons they could lay their hands upon, flourished them aloft in significant assertion that their words were but the prefaces to deeds. Again Tabarie's bull voice bellowed to those about him:

"Kings must listen to the voice of the people. Shall the man who led us to victory die a rogue's death?"

And again his thunder heralded a storm. Soldiers and citizens alike seemed prepared to rescue Villon by force from the hands of his enemies. The Scottish archers with levelled arquebusses formed a line in front of the dais and every courtier drew his sword. Only the king seemed unmoved, only the king seemed entertained by the wind he had sowed, the whirlwind he had reaped. He asked quite quietly:

"Does Master François Villon ask his life?"

Villon shook his head.

"No, sire. Master François Villon played and Master François Villon pays."

As he spoke the angry people, swaying like a sea, shouted new shouts of rescue, clamoured new cries for pardon. Olivier, green-pale, whispered eagerly to the king:

"Sire, the rogues are in a damnable temper. Can you not gain time, postpone, promise?"

Louis answered imperturbably:

"Are the fools so fond of the fellow? I know a way to stop their shouting."

As he spoke, for the first time he rose from his seat, a frail, small, black figure, to dominate those raging waves of humanity, while Olivier, holding up his hand to order silence, shouted:

"Peace, peace! The king would speak with his good people of Paris."

The noisy voices dropped slowly into silence to hear what the king said.

"Good people of Paris, I am no tyrant. But a king is the father of his people, and his ears can never be shut against the cries of his children. You all love this man? Hear, then, my judgment! This man's life is forfeit. Which of you will redeem it? If there be one among you ready to take Master François Villon's place on yonder gibbet, let that one speak now."

There was a brief silence as the mob began to realize the meaning of the king's words, a silence broken by angry cries.

"What does he mean? Take his place on the gallows! A trick - a trick!"

Louis grinned complacently.

"No trick, friends, but a simple bargain. Here is a man condemned to death; here is an idle gibbet. If ye prize him so highly, let one among you die for him. It has been said by the wise Apostle: 'Greater love hath no man than this, that a man lay down his life for his friends.' On my word as a king, when such a splendid volunteer is swinging at the end of yonder rope that moment Master François Villon shall go free. Come, who will slip neck in noose for the sake of a hero?"

Villon protested haughtily:

"No man shall die for me."

But, indeed, his protest was premature. The anger of the crowd dwindled into sullen clamours.

"The king laughs at us! 'Tis too much to ask."

A faint, exultant smile flickered over the king's face as he asked:

"Now, friends, where is your idol's supplement? Who will be his lieutenant, who will be heir to his heritage of a cross bar and a rope? You are not so brisk as you were. Does your devotion falter? Were you mocking me and him?"

Villon looked at the king with a kind of disdainful admiration.

"King of foxes!" he applauded, and the king heard him and smiled again.

"Tristan," he said, "go into yonder church and bring me an inch of candle."

Tristan bowed and entered the church. The king went on:

"Our royal mercy is mild, our royal mercy is patient. As it is our hope and our belief to live in history as a good and gracious sovereign, we would not have it said of us that we denied even a felon all due and reasonable opportunity."

Even while he spoke, Tristan came out of the church carrying in his hand a great gold candlestick in whose socket a little piece of candle, scarce an inch high, still was burning. He gave it into the hands of one of the soldiers of the Scottish Guard, who held it in his strong grasp and stood as immovable as a statue, while the thin faint flame pointed spear-like towards heaven in the warm and windless air.

Louis stopped and whispered to a page behind him who bowed and entered the church. Then the king spoke again to the silent, wondering crowd:

"So long as this candle burns, so long François Villon lives. If while it burns, one of you is moved to take Master Villon's place on the gallows, so much the better for Master Villon, and so much the worse for his substitute. Herald, proclaim our pleasure."

At a sign from Montjoye, the royal herald, two pursuivants stirred the air with the blast of golden trumpets. Then Montjoye spoke:

"The king's grace and the king's justice is ready to grant life and liberty to François Villon if anyone be found willing to take his place on the gallows and die his death that he may live his life!"

As Montjoye's words died away a great silence fell upon the assembled people, a silence so still and cruel that men's hearts grew cold and the warm June air seemed to be sighing over fields of ice. The king leaned over and addressed his prisoner confidentially:

"Master Villon, Master Villon, you see what human friendship means and the sweet voices of the multitude."

Villon answered boldly:

"Sire, it is no news to me that men love the dear habit of living."

Louis signalled to Montjoye.

"Proclaim again," he said; and once more the pair of pursuivants blew their trumpets and once again Montjoye made his singular proposition of pardon to the assemblage.

CHAPTER XVI

"WE SPEAK TO MEN"

It fell this time upon fresh ears, the ears of an old woman who was patiently pushing her way through the crowd in her effort to reach her humble lodging. She had succeeded in making her way to the open space as the last words of the herald's offer were being spoken, and suddenly her dulled brain caught the full significance of Montjoye's speech. Looking wildly around her, she saw where Villon stood, an armoured figure held captive, and without attempting to realize the meaning of what she beheld, she dropped her stick and tottered forward to the dais, where she fell on her knees with clasped, entreating hands.

"Sire, sire, I will die for him!"

Villon's heart leaped to his throat when he saw her.

"Mammy, mammy, go away!" he cried, and he made a vain attempt to move towards his mother, a movement instantly restrained by the crossed weapons of his captors. At the same moment Katherine de Vaucelles came out of the church door in obedience to the summons of a royal page, who had found her at her prayers, and who told her that the king desired her presence. She paused at the head of the steps in amazed survey of the crowded place and a scene that at first she could not understand.

"Who is this woman?" Louis asked, looking down at the poor old dame, who knelt before him and besought him. Olivier answered in his ear:

"The fellow's mother, sire."

A very little tenderness came into Louis' eyes, a very little tenderness trembled on his lips.

"Woman, we cannot hear you," he said. "By God's law you have given him life once and by my law you may not give him life again."

"Sire, I beseech you," Mother Villon entreated; but the king's pity was not to be purchased so.

"Take her away and use her gently," he said.

Noel le Jolys stooped to obey the king's command, but the old woman, rising to her feet, repulsed him fiercely.

"No! no!" she said. "I will not leave my son," and she flung her old body passionately upon the prisoner's neck and clasped with her lean arms his mailed shoulders.

Louis bade Montjoye proclaim for the last time, and once again the trumpets thundered and once again the cold, calm voice of Montjoye propounded the grim terms of the king's clemency.

The silence that followed was swiftly broken by; the

sweet, clear voice of a girl.

"I will," said Katherine de Vaucelles from her stand on the church steps, and on the instant all eyes were turned to the spot where the maiden stood with face as white as pear-blossom and her hands tightly clenched by her sides. She moved slowly down the steps in the dead silence and paused before the king's throne.

"I will die for him, sire," she said quietly.

From Villon's lips there came a mighty cry of "Katherine!" and a fain spot of colour rose on the king's cheeks.

"Mistress, we speak to men," he said.

Tristan pressed his great hands together.

"By St. Denis, our women seem to make the best men," he grunted.

Katherine stood, tall and proud, facing the king. Mother Villon, stirred by this heavenly interference, left her son to fall at the feet of the angel lady and kiss the hem of her garment.

Katherine spoke bravely:

"Sire, I love this man and would be proud to die for him. It may chime with your pleasure to slay him; it cannot chime with your honour to deny me. Your word is given and a king must keep his word."

The king made an impatient gesture.

"We speak to men."

Villon caught at his words.

"I speak to a woman," he cried, and gazirig passionately at his love, he called to her: "Katherine, my Katherine, death is a little thing. For love is deathless and you give me a better thing than life."

With unmoved voice, with unchanged face, Katherine persisted:

"Sire, I claim your promise."

Louis again denied her.

"We speak to men. Tristan, do your office."

At this moment the situation suddenly changed. Villon unexpectedly wrenched himself free from the control of the two soldiers beside him, whose hold had relaxed in their wonder at what was passing, and sprang towards Katherine. His act instantly inspired the hearts and hands of his sympathisers, and in a second he was caught up and encircled by a crowd of armed and determined men, who drove back the Scottish archers. Villon snatched a drawn sword from the hand of René de Montigny and held it high in the air while he shouted:

"No, by God's rood, the candle of my grace has not yet burnt to the socket! People of Paris, shall I not speak to my lover before I die?"

The place was a raving bedlam of noise and menace. The Scottish archers did not dare to make any attempt to recapture their escaped prisoner, but kept their line in front of the royal dais, while Villon stood by the side of Katherine with drawn sword, an archangel of insurrection, ready at any moment to fling the forces behind him upon his adversaries. Yet the king remained as unmoved as if he had been witnessing a puppet show. In his thin, even voice, he commanded:

"Speak to her while the candle burns, not a second longer."

With one accord, Villon's adherents drew back and Villon was left with Katherine alone in the open space.

Katherine whispered to him:

"François, will you not take life at my hands?"

Villon answered her tenderly:

"Dear child, if that crowned Judas there had taken you at your word, do you think I would have outlived you by the space of a second?"

She looked fixedly into his eyes.

"You are resolved?"

He smiled back at her.

"I am as stubborn as a mule and no pleadings will move me."

She looked over her shoulder with a shudder.

"Dearest, the candle flickers in the wind. There is a

dagger in your girdle. Slay me and yourself."

"You mean it?" he gasped, and she answered firmly:

"By God's Mother and God's Son."

A sudden, wonderful thought flashed through Villon's mind. He had won love, he could not hope to win life, but at least he might so manage as to die a soldier's death and not a knave's. He whispered to her eagerly:

"Then we will spoil old Louis' pleasure yet. Lore, will you marry me here at the foot of the gallows?"

She answered him:

"With all my heart."

Instantly he turned and left her and strode towards the throne.

"King, I crave your patience, but your sentence must tarry and turn, for I claim to marry this lady."

Louis smiled derisively.

"It is too late. Sing your neck-rhyme and have done, for your noose is too large for a wedding ring."

Villon gave him back smile for smile.

"Sire," he said, "I am a Master of Arts of the University of Paris and as such have the right in extremis to any sacrament of the church. I have lived a confirmed bachelor, but now I have a mind to change my state. Find me a priest, King Louis."

Olivier stooped to the king.

"He speaks the truth, sire. He can claim this right"

Louis leaned forward interested.

"What do you hope to gain by this?"

Villon answered calmly:

"The right to die like a soldier by the sword, not like a rogue by the rope."

A murmur of approval stirred the silent crowd, but it died away as Katherine suddenly advanced and stood, a white figure like a fair lily, between the king and Villon.

"Nay, you gain more than this. I am the Lady Katherine de Vaucelles, kinswoman of the royal house, mistress of a hundred lands, Grand Seneschale of Gascony, Warden of the Marches of Poitou. In my own domains I exercise the High Justice and the Low. This man is of humble birth, and when I marry him he becomes my vassal. Over my vassals I hold the law of life and death."

Villon dropped on his knees beside his lady.

Louis clapped his thin hands together as a man might applaud a play.

"You are a bold minion and you have a quick wit. But if you marry this gaol bird you decline to his condition. Your high titles fall from you, your great estates are forfeit to the crown and you and he must go out into exile together; the beggar woman with the beggar man."

Katherine turned to Villon where he knelt beside her.

"'Tis a little price to pay for my lover."

Villon looking up into her eyes, questioned her:

"Do you think I'm worth it, Kate? 'Tis a big price to pay for this poor anatomy."

She repeated her words.

"'Tis a little price to pay for my lover. Do you doubt me?"

Unheeded a man-at-arms pushed his way through the crowd to the king's dais and whispered some words in the ear of Noel le Jolys, who in turn whispered in the ear of Olivier and Olivier hearing, grew paler than before. Villon caught Katherine by the hand.

"No, Kate, no! The world is wide, our hearts are light. For a star has fallen to me from heaven and it fills the earth with glory."

His words fell on the king's ears like the voice of an oracle. Standing in his place with staring eyes and trembling fingers, he repeated falteringly the mystic words.

"A star has fallen from heaven. My dream, my dream!"

Olivier plucked at his mantle, whispering with twitching lips:

"My liege, this story spreads like the plague in the city and every alley vomits mutiny."

Louis pushed him aside.

"Rub your pale cheeks," he said; "for all is well. Destiny has spoken."

Then leaning over and stretching his thin hand towards the crowd, he cried:

"People of Paris, that man shall have his life; this woman her lover. I have tried a man's heart and found it pure gold; a woman's soul and found it all angel. True man and true woman, to each other's arms!"

And Katherine and Villon obeyed the king.

EPILOGUE

At about this point in his narrative, Dom Gregory, as those happy few who are familiar with his manuscript in the Abbey of Bonne Aventure are aware, diverges from the full current of his story to indulge in some philosophical reflections upon the character of Louis XI.

What, Dom Gregory asks in cautious interrogation, were the real intentions of the monarch with regard to François Villon and the Lady Katherine de Vaucelles? His enemies no doubt assert that he played with their destinies for a purely malignant purpose and was only prevented from carrying his evil intentions into effect by the storm of popular indignation that threatened him. Others, again, who pretend to a more intimate acquaintance with the shifty character of the king, insist that he did indeed purpose to send Master Villon to the gallows, or at least and worse, into a beggar's exile, but that lie was stayed by Master Villon's happy use of the phrase concerning a star fallen from heaven, which words, harping upon the superstitious wits of his majesty, made him believe that the dream which had puzzled him was interpreted and fulfilled. In this regard Dom Gregory records with a sly gravity how many suggest that Master François used those words of set purpose with the very intention of playing upon the strained strings of the king's mind. But there be those, too, Dom Gregory adds, and we gather from his manner that he is inclined to include himself in their number, there be those partisans of the king who maintain that the king's cruelty was from the start a mere mask for clemency, that he only intended a little malicious sport with the too outspoken lover and the too disdainful lass, and that it had never been in the scope of his thoughts seriously to punish either the broker of ballads or the valiant maid of Vaucelles.

Starting from this point, Dom Gregory indulges in a great many reflections upon kings and kingship and the consequences of kingly acts, all of which seemed perhaps more momentous at the time when they were written and in the sleepy Abbey where they lie enshrined, than in busier and more bustling times. One could have wished that Dom Gregory had let such philosophies go by the board and had given us instead some greater knowledge of what happened to François Villon and Katherine de Vaucelles after they fell upon each other's necks in that open place in Paris, with the mob huzzahing, the king staring and Tristan's strange satellites busily dismantling the useless gibbet. But here Dom Gregory is little less than dumb. Losses in the manuscript account for much of his silence; perhaps his ecclesiastical indifference to the wedded state may account for more. If we can gather vaguely from other sources that the poet and his mistress settled down on a small and quiet estate in Poitou, lived a peaceful country life for many years and died a peaceful country death at the end, it is the most we can hope to gain with surety. We are glad to believe in their happiness, for he was a true lover and she was a fair woman.

Justin Huntly McCarthy

www.ingramcontent.com/pod-product-compliance
Lightning Source LLC
Chambersburg PA
CBHW050037180626
46810CB00002B/771